Tears from Brabant

Auguste van der Molenschot

TEARS FROM BRABANT

A novel

Aspekt Publishers

Tears from Brabant

Original Dutch title: Brabantse Tranen © 2017 ASPEKT Publishing
© 2018 Aspekt Publishers
© Auguste van der Molenschat

Translation: © Auguste van der Molenschot

Aspekt Publishers | Amersfoortsestraat 27
3769 AD Soesterberg | The Netherlands
info@uitgeverijaspekt.nl | www.uitgeverijaspekt.nl

Photo front cover: Jos Droog Fotografie, Hilvarenbeek, 2017
Photo back cover: Vught Castle
Cover design: Britt Ouwehand/ Thomas Wunderink
Lay-out: Brigitte de Graaf

ISBN: 9789463385169
NUR: 300

Disclaimer – The author and the publisher have made every feasible effort to determine and acquire copyright permissions for material presented in this book. If any right-holders have been overlooked we kindly request them to apply to the publisher.

*More people hate me for no reason
than I have hairs on my head
More are groundlessly hostile
than I have hair to show
They ask me to give back what I never took*

(the Jerusalem Bible, Doubleday 1966, The Psalms 69:4)

Contents

Preface to this English language translation		9
Foreword		12
I	Altar Boy	15
II	The Seventh Cardinal Sin	33
III	Lotte and her Ma	37
IV	Higher Calling, War and Sex	43
V	Going Steady?	51
VI	Creaking Marriage	58
VII	My Romantic Soul	62
VIII	Full Professor	65
IX	My Opa	67
X	Murder?	74
XI	Brabant and the Brabanter	76
XII	Great Grandfather, Grandfather, Father	84
XIII	Willibrord and Later	88
XIV	The Block	90
XV	HBS and Military Service	93
XVI	St. Augustine	99
XVII	Studying and no Sex	103
XVIII	Lotte	106
XIX	Engaged?	108
XX	Break-up	114
XXI	Verona and Thereafter	117
XXII	Professor B.	124
XXIII	Again Together	127
XXIV	Doctoral, but not Really	130
XXV	No Love	133
XXVI	Prozac	136

XXVII	Unfaithful?	142
XXVIII	Married	144
XXIX	Enigma	149
XXX	Breaking Marriage	155
XXXI	Niels Stensen	158
XXXII	The Loge and Emigration	162
XXXIII	Hypocritical Pharisee	166
XXXIV	Canada the First Time Around	172
XXXV	Ma's Reincarnation	174
XXXVI	The Ultimatum	179
XXXVII	The Compromise	186
XXXVIII	Incest	189
XXXIX	La Douce France	194
XL	Male Chauvinist Pig	196
XLI	The Opus Dei Weekend	203
XLII	Sick and Ill	209
XLIII	Handicapped	215
XLIV	Calgary and Prozac	225
XLV	Catatonic	229
XLVI	Fighting Pain	232
XLVII	Adultery	235
XLVIII	Intermission	239
XLIX	Murder after All?	241
L	The Attack	245
LI	Divorce	248
LII	Leaving Home	254
LIII	Depression	256
LIV	Sandra	260
LV	Hanne	262
LVI	Jacob	266
LVII	Hanne's Death	270
LVIII	On to The Hague	274
LIX	After the Dunning Letter	279
LX	Revenge	285

Preface to the English-language translation.

What is Brabant? What is a Brabanter and how is he/she different from other people? Chapters XI-XIII deal with these questions, but more importantly perhaps this novel is throughout infused with that Brabanter feeling.

For the uninitiated here a brief discourse of history. The Netherlands as it is presently, is only part of a greater Netherlands, called "The Low Countries" (les Pays Bas in French and Los Países Bajos in Spanish). It comprised the Netherlands, Belgium, Luxembourg and the North-West corner of France called "Picardy". By contrast, "Holland" refers only to the Provinces of North- and South-Holland and perhaps part of Zeeland. For a long time the Low Countries were part of the Spanish Empire. In the 16th century North-West Netherlands fought themselves free from the Spaniards and almost simultaneously converted to the Calvinist brand of Protestantism. The dividing line was formed by "the Great Rivers" meaning the delta of the rivers Maas, Waal and Rhine. South of that line lay "Brabant", still Spanish and still Catholic in the main. After the defeat of Napoleon the greater Netherlands was created by the Conference of Vienna in 1815, with Prince William VI of Orange being appointed to rule over this area as King William I. He was an absolute Monarch and long did his rule not last. The Southern (Catholic) areas revolted, leading to a civil war in 1830 and the official creation of Belgium in 1839. The area known as Brabant ended up split in two over two countries, the Northern part becoming eventually the Province of North Brabant of the new (reduced) State of the Netherlands.

Brabant as a geographical and political entity was first created by Duke Jan of Brabant (1254 - 1294). He brought stability and prosperity. Culture flourished. The capital of Brabant was (and is) Brussels. At the time of Charles Quint (1500-1558) Brussels was the luxurious capital of Europe. The iconic polyptich painting by the Van Eyck brothers "The Adoration of the Mystic Lamb" was painted there 220 years before Rembrandt painted his "Night Watch". Renaissance (and indeed civilization) came to Holland only by way of Brabant. The many 15th century churches one still finds in Holland are all in a style called "Brabant Gothic". Who were these Brabant people? In the main they were Frankish groups that had come from Germany and who then (scared away by those mighty rivers), had turned Southwards to eventually create France. They came under control of the Roman Empire. With these legions came also Christian teachers and these Frankish 'heathens' converted readily to Christianity (later called Roman Catholicism). North of the great rivers the ethnicity was mainly Saxon and Frisian (= Angel). 1500 years later the (North) Brabanters were caught in a vise that held them imprisoned as virtual slaves for almost three centuries. Their religion remained forbidden. They had almost no civil rights: no voting rights, therefore no representation, no passports even, no access to good schools or to certain jobs such as in the civil service and to many professions (judges, professors). Officially this discrimination ended in 1853 when the Netherlands arrived at a Concord with the Vatican: an agreement that allowed for freedom of religion. Bishops, priests and nuns were again allowed in, churches were built. Unfortunately, more·than a century later the emancipation of the Catholics in the Netherlands still was not complete. This novel, while it follows the career of a Catholic Brabanter in the 20th century, recounts the discrimination he still had to endure. He lived the discrimination that was an everyday part of his life. Not only because of these protestant Hollanders but also because his own parents, his own people, his own bishops told him to always keep his head down. He did not and he won, only to lose it all in the end. And yet he won again, by never bending. To quote Henry Miller:

I have no money, no resources, no hope
I am the happiest man alive

Foreword

Language is the foundation of civilization. This I heard already early in my young life and I have lived constantly according to that mantra. It began with reading anything and everything I could get my hands on and at the time that meant a maximum of three books a week from the Public Library. Soon I started also writing; about from the fourth year of the primary school onwards. I never looked back. Initially just writing exercises at school, later scientific papers about sometimes extremely esoteric subjects. At the same time also poetry, short stories and serious essays. Of these, the essays are dearest to my heart, in spite of the fact that they generated little public interest. Why this preference? Because in these essays the smallness and the greatness of human activities may be shown in symbiotic combination. "You are really a story teller", someone told me recently. Maybe so, I thought, but why was it then so difficult to write a novel? Only now my debut as a novelist and indeed it was a difficult delivery. No 800 or 1400 words as we see so often nowadays in serious literature. Rather very compact, with many flashbacks and flashforwards as indeed we do in our thinking process. With indeed that symbiosis of the great with the tiny. With at every turn that major red thread of Love. No autobiography but rather a mixture of experiences with pure fiction. A composed story which, I hope, will keep the reader spellbound till the end.

Many assisted me in this joyful endurance test. Many times major changes were made, forcing me to start all over. Curiously, I started off in English, only to be told that first I should complete a Dutch version. Which I did with "*Brabantse Tranen*" which appeared in September 2017. Now back to my second first language, roughly translating from the Dutch version. To all my friends and readers of the first and later hours my great thanks. And finally, a dedication: to the girl with the golden locks.

The author and translator

I

Altar Boy

The first time I became a man I was only seven years old. I had done my best at school so that at the end of my first year I could read almost anything. My maternal grandmother, whom we called *Opoe,* had come up with the idea that I should perhaps become an altar boy. *Opoe* lived in an old folks home run by the Sisters of Love, a Roman Catholic Congregation of Nuns. She lived there, quite decently, in the second class. She did not belong to the upper class; that was only for the very rich ladies and third class no, that was only for the poor. About these poor I will tell more, later on. My *Opoe* owned two little houses and from the rental income from these she could live quite nicely. She had a drawing room and a separate bedroom and therefore she earned also a modicum of respect with the Sisters. Her proposal was therefore listened to and lo and behold, it was accepted. I was going to become an altar boy! At the bookstore where they also sold office supplies I purchased the altar boy Mass manual and I bought a sheet of black wrapping-paper. This was to serve as a cover for that manual and my mother took it upon her to cover my manual. Then, with that holy booklet in my hands, I went to my room.

Confiteor Deo Omnipotenti
I confess to You, my Almighty God

And so it went on, heavy going for a boy of seven. However, it got much worse:

Mea culpa, mea culpa, mea maxima culpa
Through my fault, through my fault, through my greatest fault

It did not say anywhere what my culpability really was. For the time being I was to take it for granted that I was a sinner; why this was so would be explained later. It was a bit like *Sinterklaas*. That the *Sint* could walk across the roof tops was quite acceptable; he was holy after all! He lived in Heaven but once and a while he came down to Earth. Jesus had done the same so that was not very special. Whenever the *Sint* was on Earth he lived in Spain amidst his helpers and then, in December, he arrived in the Netherlands with shiploads of presents for us all. At all times he rode a white horse, but it was beyond me why this horse would not fall off the roof tops. I was told that this was a Secret of the Faith that would be explained to me in the Hereafter. By the time you did no longer have to believe in *Sinterklaas* anymore, that mystical secret only became larger. Later, much later, several religious crises later and with a quite different understanding of God, it would all become clearer to me. However, the mystical white horse kept after me for decades to come, being it that it would arrive in different disguises.

I had assumed that I had to learn the entire manual by heart immediately; however, my mother put me to bed while it was still light. The next morning I would have to get up at 6 AM and then go to the Sisters without breakfast. Everybody there would take Communion and therefore you were not to eat or drink after midnight. Not even brush your teeth! Of course, in the chapel there was a second, experienced altar boy and in the first couple of weeks all I had to do was to murmur along. Soon, however, came the day that I was the *numero uno* and it even happened that I was the only altar boy and that was exciting because I then had to do double service. Strangely enough I could do it without fail. How on earth was this possible? A child, a little boy who could scarcely tie his shoe laces and who could not even repair a leaking bicycle tire! Most of the times such solo altar boy performances went without a hitch and then I received compliments from Sister Sacristy and sometimes even a nickel or two from the priest. To make one thing clear; I never have been sexually assaulted by whatever priest, brother or nun. Never even noticed or heard anything of that nature from other altar boys. In the meantime I had become part of something absolutely grand. Here was this little boy, eight years old by now and he was leading the Greatest Show on Earth! Because that was exactly how it felt. Everything depended on me. The priest could only start when I brought him the wine and the water. And I had to ring the altar bells and the large wall-mounted Consecration bell at the right times. Then, during Mass at the festive days, I had to prepare the incense burner. Oh, that heavenly smell! A little piece of char coal had to keep the incense smoldering in just the right manner; not too fierce and not too lifeless. By the time I handed the incense burner to the priest he should be able to immediately produce deliciously smelling clouds. On other moments it befell on us, altar boys, to swing the censer. Ah, what a wonderful feeling it was to be a Catholic!

To tell the truth, I could do far more than I realized myself. I could by now read and therefore gain access to everything that had been written and printed. At home there was the daily newspaper and also the Catholic Illustration. My mother subscribed to *Beatrijs* (a women's biweekly), but that magazine I was not allowed to read. Later I understood why. This magazine contained also ads for ladies underwear and looking at these ads would not have been wholesome for my young innocent soul. On the other hand, I could look, observe and be curious about everything around me and I could store all these – mostly ill-understood – data into my brains. These intellectual abilities were still in their infancy, but they were there, quite clearly. Obvious perhaps to the outside observer, while I was mostly oblivious to it all. To me it was like a tsunami, a furious onslaught of a process that engulfed me, the process of growing up, of becoming a man.

Much of this played out in a chapel that made my romantic heart beat faster, every time I entered it. Much later I would see and experience the *Sainte Chapelle* in Paris, An absolute high and reference point of West European gothic architecture. To me, however, the chapel of the Sisters of Love, built in Brabantine late-gothic, was barely inferior. High ogive windows with stained glass windows, showing a variety of biblical scenes, an altar with a wood-cut triptych, a tabernacle with a sculptured door of pure gold, the lower altar and steps in many-colored marble. I absorbed all this in all its detail but without critical analysis. It made a great impression on me with images forever engraved on the retinas, still long before I could put such feelings into words.

We, altar boys, were also beautifully attired. There were the day-to-day black togas but also the red ones for festive days. Even light blue togas for the Maria feasts. There were altar bells in kinds; I preferred the silver ones with their high-toned light-footed sound. Where was all this richness coming from? From legacies, from gifts from the inhabitants or from their inheritors, and sometimes from the families of the nuns themselves. In the chapel the wealthiest of the inhabitants would sit up-front, sometimes in their private luxurious praying chair. How could it have been differently? Then, behind the first class inhabitants, the Teaching Sisters. Well educated and equipped with Teaching College degrees, they were real ladies, who would bring in much money; their State-paid teaching salaries would flow directly into the bank account of the convent. Behind them the nuns with special tasks and functions such as Mother Superior, Sister Fiscal, Sister Music, our own Sister Sacristy, the Care Sisters in charge of the kitchen, vegetable garden and stable, Sister Nurse and so on. Behind them the second class inhabitants. Finally, there were the Sisters whom we called the Cleaning and Swabbing Sisters but amongst them also the lower staff of the kitchen *et cetera*. However, the latter group was not to be found in the main chapel. These were nuns who under lighter or greater pressure of their parents had been dumped into a convent for a variety of reasons. They were considered superfluous in the outside world; perhaps too ugly to ever catch a husband, or too dumb to do any useful work, or mentally or physically slightly handicapped, they were given a life of labor in a convent. Where would they sit? Well, you see, this beautiful chapel had a side aisle, almost invisible from the main aisle, all for the third class paupers plus these lower caste nuns. Ranks there have to be. God did not create all humans equal and did they ever believe this.

Yeah, that third class. I ought to tell a bit more about it, be it with a troubled heart. Those were the poor people, the old folks who had nothing and who could not work for money anymore. Old-age pensions did exist here and there but not for everybody. And if you then had no savings or other sources of income where else could you turn? Beautiful tradition of the Church to look after these poor, as She had been doing already for some twenty centuries. Indeed they got a roof, meals, a warm bed and that was about it. This young altar boy knew the third class section fairly well, although this part of the convent complex was almost entirely separated from the other parts. The third class had its own entry door, actually a small, nondescript back door. Whenever I visited my *Opoe*, I often used a short cut. I left through an unmarked door in the second class section, passing then through the third class. I descended a stair to arrive on a little inner court where these unfortunates would sit.

On such occasions I sometimes encountered a nun; I was recognized as one of the altar boys so the nun would perhaps make some small talk but essentially they let me pass without interference. Sometimes I would even talk with one or another third classer and even that raised no comment. In these contacts I noticed something that filled me with amazement. There were separate areas for men and women. In itself already remarkable in that in the first and second class there were only women, widows mostly and a few old spinsters. Were there then no widowers? Yes, but not many. As a man you simply died at a younger age than a woman. The few widowers either remarried quickly or they would engage a live-in house keeper. If you had no financial resources than you could as man also knock on the door of the Sisters of Love. They would welcome you, strip you of your last savings, in order to next place you with the other men of no means. However, that was not only the standard protocol for poor single persons but also for the poor married couples!

I knew full well what the Church had to say about Holy Matrimony. Marriage was a saintly institution and: "What God has united, no men can separate". The Church still does not recognize divorce or any other way of ending a marriage apart from death. However, here in this convent, the Sisters of Love acted completely contrary to Church Law by separating men and women, even when they were a married couple. During the day time there was a short happy hour when they were allowed to meet each other in this courtyard or perhaps in parts of the garden. I still have an image on my retina of this old couple sitting on a little bench next to each other. Somehow she has procured a sweet mint which she has kept for her husband. Full of pride and joy she gives it to him and watches him smilingly and with gleaming eyes as he puts the sweet into his mouth sucking it with evident pleasure. Was this the Love that Jesus had preached? Definitely between these two old people, but what about the nuns with their rules and regulations? Was this not an attitude of utter lack of love? Later, much later, I asked an old retired nun about it. She confirmed that this was indeed the rule in all homes for the poor. "And not just in the Catholic ones", she added apologetically. "Ach", she said, "we did not want anything having to do with that dirty stuff", referring to sexual contacts, should you not already have guessed it. Later again I discovered that such was indeed also the rule in Protestant and secular homes for the poor. Talking about the sanctity of marriage!

Via that courtyard I would reach the back door of the convent complex, which actually opened to the playground of the adjoining girls schools which were also run by the nuns. Even when the German Occupier took over those schools during WWII, I was still allowed to use that rear exit.

Forty years later I made a kind of pilgrimage to the neighborhood of my early youth. I was surprised to come upon a huge pile of rubble. The entire convent, complete with the schools and my beloved chapel had been bulldozed. Nothing was left of the old glory, in order to make room for a new-to-be-built secular care complex for seniors. The nuns had left, never to return. The major reason was the strongly diminished influx of young new nuns. And then the project developers are quick to move in as vultures to pick over the bones.

Filled with sadness I walked away from this heap of broken bricks, towards the nearby cemetery. I used to go to that cemetery quite often, visiting the graves of my grandparents and then already some of my aunts and uncles. I found such visits always very uplifting. Here I made contact with the Community of the Departed as the Church likes to call it. I then visualized how they had been and I happily anticipated to meet them again after the Day of Reckoning. But then, confusion! Where was the cemetery? Was I getting lost? Gone, totally gone and in its place a new housing development had been built. And what had they then done with the remains of my family members and of all those other families? One person quickly informed me: "Oh, yes, that is how it goes nowadays. The bones were dug up to be burned in the destructor oven and then the land was sold for redevelopment".

Where this reminded me of? World War II had left our family almost totally untouched. No one had died a violent death. Now the ashes of my family members had ended up in little tin cans after all. Unbelievable! Forgive me Lord if now some heavyweight words come to mind, words I never use in my language. How could they do this? Is there no longer any respect for our Elders, our Dead? While I write these words, I cannot prevent the tears from coming to my eyes.

The status of my *Opoe* was also enhanced by my becoming an altar boy. People whispered: "Who is that new altar boy?" "Oh, he is one from Annie from Huberdina from Huupkes, you know". In Brabant people seldom used surnames; that was a novelty introduced by Napoleon and they still had not yet gotten used to it. At home my status had also increased. Suddenly I was someone to be reckoned with. The alarm clock had to be set, I got nice new clothes; I was suddenly a news item. Aunts and uncles heard about it and when I next told them that I wanted to become Pope then not infrequently I got a dime or so for my piggy bank. At school it was no different. Normally I had plenty of time for breakfast and to be on time for school after having served the 7 AM Mass. However, sometimes there was a Mass that would start much later, like with a burial. Then I would be too late at school with the best possible excuse: "I had to serve a Mass, Master". Master would accept that excuse without question and the boys in my class then also knew it: I was an altar boy!

Then suddenly, something extremely important and of great consequence happened: war broke out in our country. No-one was allowed in the streets before 7 AM, but I was exempted! The streets were pitch black dark; there were no street lights anymore and all houses and other buildings were completely darkened by black paper covering all windows and even filling up small holes or slits. The streets themselves were completely desolate; no pedestrians, no bicycles and not even a single automobile. In the evening, members of the Air Protection Service of each town would patrol to make sure nowhere even the slightest bit of light was escaping. Woe on anyone trespassing! These people, mostly volunteers, were responsible for the air safety of their town; they were also in charge of the Air-raid Alarms with their frightening sirens. On moonlit nights with a clear sky you could see quite well where you were going; your eyes would adapt to the available light from the moon and the stars. However, in the long winter nights with new moon and overcast skies it could really be pitch dark. Quite literally you then could not see the hands of your outstretched arms. This young boy had to find his way by groping at the brick and mortar of the houses. At some point, though, the houses stopped and then I had to cross a rather wide street, hoping that I could maintain my direction in the dark until I felt the curb of the walkway at the other side. Then again gropingly a little further until I could feel the wrought iron fencing of the convent. At the door Sister Door appeared as a black shadow in a black frame, allowing me through in silence.

My altar boy career lasted only two years. My parents had decided to move to another neighborhood in our town. Different school, different parish and I was not allowed to remain altar boy with the nuns, never mind that I pleaded that I could easily walk those 15 extra minutes. Somehow I had gained in self-confidence and I rang the doorbell of the new parish priest and asked to speak the *pastoor,* the head of the priests. Indeed he received me and he asked who I was and about my family and so on. The end result was zero. I had noticed already that the altar boys in my class were all from the well-to-do families. I had nobody to speak for me and therefore I never got in. The new school also caused its problems. Indeed there was a rich corner in this neighborhood but for the most it was a blue collar area. There you had to fight to gain your place in the hierarchy. And fighting, that was an absolute no-no with my parents. My glasses might break. And those glasses I needed very badly at school. Replacing broken glasses would take weeks if not months. It was war, remember! So I asked the leader of this gang if I could first take off my glasses and then they could beat me as much as they wanted. That indeed they did but after one or two of these beating sessions their enjoyment had ebbed away and they let me be. From then on they called me *brillejood* (= jew-boy with glasses).

So started my Great Loneliness as permanent indictment. Once proud, I had been toppled from my pedestal. I became that solitary, who belonged nowhere. It absolutely was no help that I had excellent brains and made high marks at school in all subjects; quite to the contrary. Fortunately there was a Roman Catholic Public Library and there I borrowed the maximum of three books each week. However, I had longed to play soccer, just like all other boys and I had longed for a special friend. "Never mind", said my mother, "do stay home to read your book or to make that jig-saw puzzle. Those boys are no good for you anyhow". My mother had a very strongly developed sense of rank. She distinguished between at least twenty societal levels. That had also already been so at our previous address. "No, his father is a *stempelaar* (= an unemployed who had to present himself every day at city hall to receive a stamp mark in his employment booklet). That kind of folks is nothing for us". Or: "Those people are not Catholic". Or:

"No, don't play with that son of our doctor anymore. You might get uppity ideas from that". My father was a lower white collar worker; unfortunately in our street there were no more of those lower bourgeoisie people. Not in our earlier place and not at our new address. My mother never said: "Come here", to give me a warm hug. That simply never happened. My mother had a husband and four sons and not even a single daughter. That latter point was one of her great regrets in life. I think that she never was comfortable with all those male bodies at home.

My mother had endured her own personal problems, but at that time I had absolutely no inkling of that. Much later, especially after she had become a widow, she began to spill her stories to me. My mother was of course of an older generation, born in the early years of the 20th century. *Opoe* had raised her daughters in the 'proper' way. At that epoch 'proper' meant 'total ignorance'. In that state my mother had entered marriage, not knowing, not even suspecting that a male body looked different from her own. Had she then not received any (sexual) information and instructions? Oh, yes! In preparation towards her marriage the *pastoor* had called her in and he had said: "I assume that you know all about it?" My mother had nodded: "Yes *pastoor*", although she had not had the slightest idea what the man was referring to. The Sheppard had added: "In that case I have nothing to add, except to say that you should take care that no seed is lost". And once more my mother had answered that she had understood although she thought that he had been referring to canaries. With that kind of sexual education she had been sent home. Did she never notice then anything? Was she that naïve? After all, she had four brothers and were these not different from her sisters? Yes, but that again was hidden as much as possible. On Mondays she helped her mother with the weekly laundry, but the underpants of the men she never got to see. These were laundered separately by her mother and when they were hung on the drying line, a bedsheet was thrown across it so that my mother would never notice that these underpants were different!

At one point her oldest brother Jan, already married, had gotten his first child. Naturally my mother had gone to visit and to see the baby. She had heard that it was a little boy and that his name would be Hubert. She then had this bright idea and she had asked: "Tell me Jan, how did you know that it was a boy?" "Well, that is easy", her brother had answered, "boys have wool under their feet". And my mother had happily replied that she now understood. My mother then was 22 years of age and already engaged; shortly thereafter she herself would enter a marriage that indeed would endure till their last days.

I never got a hug, I never felt a tender stroke along my cheek, there never was a loving word. I did not know that I belonged to the group of HSP people. In fact that word, meaning Highly Sensitive Person, did not even exist for much of my life. It means that certain people are sensitive, sometimes extremely sensitive for their environment, for people, plants and animals. I not only longed for a hug, I realized that I was also capable of giving that kind of love. Yes, giving such tender loving became a need for my sensitive soul. Had my mother been a bad mother? Of course not! My mother did everything possible to keep her nuclear family going and bringing up these sons. Even if she had to play father and mother at the same time. In particular during the war much had to be improvised. My father had had a very smart idea. Immediately upon becoming Occupied Country he had purchased 2000 of the finest Willem II cigars. He had hidden them under the floor of the living room, keeping them dry in a special heated box. Now, in 1943 and 1944, these cigars became excellent trading material in the black market. They could also be sold at high prices; towards the end a single 6-cent cigar would fetch 4-5 guilders, about a weekly gage of a manual laborer. Trading was less dangerous, though, and my mother soon excelled at it. On the sandy soil of Brabant only rye and potatoes could be grown. My mother soon found a farmer who, against the gift of a box of 10 cigars, filled our cellar with a year's supply of potatoes, plus that every 2-4 weeks he sold us 25 kg of rye. That rye grain had to be milled into rye meal by the blacksmith (against a percentage of course), but even so, my parents would bake two large rye bread loafs twice a week. A welcome and even vital addition to the official meager rations. It was considerably more difficult to find butter or bacon, because our farmers barely had any themselves. There was no feed for the cows, so these had to live off the land and in Brabant that was not so easy. Milk or cheese was not to be found at any price. However, my mother with one or two boxes with cigars safely hidden in her underwear got onto her bicycle, past all kinds of control posts and then she would come home with an unspeakably delicious pound of real butter or a side of bacon. Shoes were a different matter; there were ration coupons for shoes, but the shoe shops were simply empty most of the time. On a certain day my mother got onto her bicycle again to go downtown to a shoe shop. She knew nobody there but she announced that she wanted shoes for her four sons. Whether she had any coupons for that, she was asked. "No", said my mother and she opened her overcoat, "but I have these", showing the boxes with cigars she had hidden there. "Ah", said the slightly taken aback salesman, "I will call the boss". She was called into the office of the owner and soon the deal was made. It was very risky what my mother did there. If either the salesman or the owner had been a Nazi sympathizer she would have lost her entire trading supply plus a substantial fine if not jail. With clothing it was a similar refrain. When her own mother died – our *Opoe* - , she came home with a load of white bedsheets, which were transformed by her into dress shirts for her husband and the four sons. Wool from old sweaters were recycled into socks. About my mother you could say that she lived in a small world. She lived for her family, never took any holidays and bought for herself only new clothes when the old ones were worn out. She had no hobbies and she was not a member of any organization except perhaps for that Catholic Illustration and the *Beatrijs* women's magazine. She transferred her shortcomings to her children, that is certainly true, but how could she have done otherwise? I wanted to go to a totally different world; a world that she did not know and therefore was suspicious of. Logical that she did not trust the aspirations of her third son. However, I always honored my mother, her always addressing with the formal "Thou".

My father really was a strange bird. Perhaps the best characteristic is that he was extremely shy and unworldly. He would never enter the black or grey market in search of food the way my mother did. He would never attend PTA events at my school; my mother forced herself to do just that once and a while. Where she heard things which somehow frightened and unsettled her. Such as that this child was highly gifted and that she should not worry. Plus that he most certainly should go on in higher learning. Once and a while my father did something rather unexpected, showing an initiative like purchasing those 2000 cigars while everyone said that the war would be over by Christmas. He also purchased several 10 kg heavy sugar loaves which also were stored underneath the living room. For his wife he bought a *Miele* electric washing machine, probably the last one available in town. For himself and with his last savings he bought the *Rolleycord* camera that he had long wanted. In the new home he built a dark room so that he could develop and print his own photos. Marvelous when I was asked to help him. In the almost-dark I handed him the tools and materials he needed or I had to move and shake the developing tanks until the images would appear, first weakly and then stronger and sharper! He also taught himself to become a gardener, so that we could grow some vegetables and fruits of our own. Much needed in wartime! My father could repair bicycles, he was an accomplished book binder and he could swim. With him

I biked large distances through the fields and forests, but also all through our town. I think that I inherited my continual sense of curiosity from him. My father did not have much formal education and he soon became aware that intellectually I was outgrowing him, even while I was still a child. Occasionally that led to some friction or collisions. I did my best to avoid these, in the meantime thinking of how to leave home as soon as possible. My father was a good accountant and when I finally left home he soon discovered the fiscal advantages thereof. To begin with, he cashed in on double child support and on top he claimed triple child deduction on his income tax because I was a university student. At the same time I paid my living expenses and studying expenses entirely by myself, so my father enriched himself considerably. Without even thinking about it he pocketed all that money; it did not even occur to him that these funds were actually for me. And I then? To me it did not even occur to approach my father on this topic let alone to take him to account for his actions. Much later it occurred to me that he changed his car for a new one quite often: "There goes my Child Support", I thought sometimes. However, my father too I respected for what he was and did; I also addressed him always as "Thou".

II

The Seventh Cardinal Sin

"Gus, may I give you Absolution?"

"Am I a sinner, then?"

"Oh, yes, and a heavy duty one even. You got stuck with one of the seven cardinal sins and of these even the worst one. Do you not know that you are extremely proud? There is no God in the world and certainly not ours, who will put such a burden on your shoulders as you now are carrying. What are you doing there, with all that guilt and responsibility you have taken on your shoulders? Of course it is killing you. Man, for God's sake, start loving yourself a bit".

"And what about Job then", I interjected? However, my *pastoor* and spiritual guide did not let go:

"Job knew that his trials had been planted there by his God and that is why he could endure them. He knew that these burdens would never be beyond his capacity to carry them and therefore he never gave up. However, you Gus, with your pride you are taking too much on your shoulders. As strong as you indeed are, you will break if you do not soon start living and thinking differently".

And that was the message I had to swallow. I asked some time for the matter of absolution. Not only did I have to get used to the idea, it was necessary that I would totally absorb the idea that I was a sinner.

In the meantime it was sixty years later. I already belonged to the seniors and I still had not grasped why everything had so utterly gone wrong in my life, in spite of my good intentions and my enormous efforts. However, perhaps I was now on the proper track. That sentence: "Go and start loving yourself", I had heard once before, about three years earlier. At that time already I had promised myself to really do something about it. Then perhaps the understanding would come and with it the acceptance.

I had been at wits end and I had really considered that perhaps it was all not true and that I was living in a set of delusional brain warps. What had happened to me, at least what I thought had happened to me, was so absurd to border on the unbelievable. I also considered that all these fast loves I had had recently ought to have a deeper meaning. Why was it that my half-life with the ladies suddenly only was only 3-6 months? I would then have been really in love. I did my best to win the other and to create something beautiful out of this relation. That worked for a while and then the decline began. Then the shortcomings of the other would push themselves to the fore, next to all my own ones. Doubts would emerge; could I really manage this? Would I have the flexibility in order to be tolerant and be openminded to the other, who turned out to be so totally different? The other also had a rucksack full of past life with a shopping list of desirable items to overcome it all.

Much had happened to me in the intervening years. An absurd marriage, followed by a divorce and after that a new splendid new relation. Unfortunately this relation ended by death through a tumor in the brains of my beloved. Was that perhaps also my fault? Had that great mutual Love perhaps been too large? Is there a limit to the measure of Love that a human can tolerate? Perhaps too great a Love is not meant to exist for mankind, at least not for most or at least not here on Earth. Hanne's death had affected me deeply. At long last – I was already 64 years old – a woman had said to me: "Gus, I love you". For the first time in my life I had heard these heavenly words. She had undressed and nakedly she had come to me to embrace me. After her death it seemed so logical to seek a successor. Of course I wanted to feel that love again. That is where it all went wrong and I had fallen into a crisis. I looked for help and I found a married couple psychologist-psychiatrist and to that I added a psychotherapist. To this team I said: "Here I am. Turn me inside out if you wish, but please, tell me what is wrong with me".

The result was rather sobering: "We have listened to your story, Gus. Everything you have told us is true, nothing is imagined. Of course, it is not the entire truth, but this is how you have experienced it, and nothing of it is untrue. Your story is so absurd that you or anyone could not possibly have imagined it. And even if you had, we would have caught you in no time flat in your own net of fantasies. Remember, we are used to see all kinds of liars, psychotics, simulants, schizophrenics, and cunning manipulators. You are none of these. Of course, we tried to trip you. But then you replied in a way that seamlessly fitted your earlier words, and in such a way to enhance the picture that we were already building of you. You yourself had already noticed some of the red threads, such as the loneliness that was a guiding principle in your life. We discovered more of these threads. Everything had a consistency that sometimes was even hair-raising, a consistency that was nowhere broken or even challenged, not even in some detail. Psychologically speaking you, Gus, suffer from nothing. Not a single ailment or personality defect. Nothing at all. However, Gus, we worry about you nevertheless. You do have an inclination to let other people walk over you. This is a equanimity that is to be praised in general, which in your case has gone much too far. That in itself caused you lots of trouble. Definitely in the past and as far as we can see also in the present and presumably in the future. You are just a bit too nice and too sweet. Towards everyone except to yourself. You keep ignoring and self-effacing yourself, as if this is normal and required. You should work on that point, my friend, if you don't want to get caught again in one or another web. Go and love yourself also a bit, dear friend, even if it means that once and a while you have to say 'no' to someone". And that was that same advice that now I had heard again from my spiritual guide, the *pastoor*. The second time that I heard: "Go and love yourself".

III

Lotte and her Ma

To my mind she never should have been called Lotte. In the Dutch language 'to be touched by a '*lotje*', means a person is not well in the head. Quite predictably she was forever asked if she had had been touched by a *lotje*. The bad and painful part of this was that indeed she was, certainly from about her 15th year onwards.

How cruel of her parents to saddle their first-born with such a ridiculous name! Actually, she looked quite attractive. Slim but not thin, with small but firm straight protruding breasts that looked good in a Marilyn Monroe angora woolen sweater. Lower legs a bit short and a head that was a bit too large for her body, but come on, nobody is totally perfect. A thick bunch of curly golden-blond hair, framing her face and neck. When the sun shone through it, her hair sometimes looked like a golden halo. And I don't want to suggest that she had anything saintly about her. She rather looked disarming, somewhat innocent, naïve. When she dressed in a thin nylon summer dress then you would see a pair of beautiful arms of an extremely light alabaster skin color. Plenty, therefore, to make any young man's heart beat faster.

So, that is what happened to me. Not immediately, because our first meeting was far from audacious. No, that first meeting was quite forgettable. I was presented to her by a friend, whom I still knew from my first stay at Leyden. Karel was member of an executive of one of these student 'Disputes' and Lotte was also part of that executive. He had to speak to Lotte about some Dispute business and I was just tagging along. Karel rang her doorbell and then it turned out that Lotte was ill. However, she did come down in her night gown and indeed she looked very pale and wan. Later I would learn that this was not her monthly indisposition but that Lotte became ill, usually two or three times every month, throwing up her bile and then recovering somewhat till the next attack. I also learned soon that this always happened after she had spent a weekend at her parental home. Why then not just stay at Leyden? Now, that was entirely out of the question.

At the home of the Ten Brink family Ma was the undisputed King. Oops, Queen. She had decreed that Lotte should come home every weekend. Then and there Lotte would get a frontal attack, after which she could travel back to Leyden with a sorrowful heart. Ma ten Brink was fully convinced that the whole world was against her. She eternally felt underrated and shortchanged. Especially by her husband. However, he had found the effective anti-weapon. He simply never answered her and if she would become too nasty, he would get up and leave home saying that he had extra work at the office. Indeed he often made extra hours but the question was whether that was only to make some extra money for his too-large family of seven children. So,

Ma next complained to her eldest daughter Lotte who heard nothing but negative comments about her. "You better go to University and get a degree because you will never get a husband. Look at that frumpy dress you are wearing. You have absolutely no taste. You, you cannot even boil a potato". Later she would add other complaints: "All of you, you give me no respect. I am always shortchanged here. And uncle Jan was also so unfriendly to me recently and also last year during his birthday visit. And aunt Els is going on holiday again; how can they afford it and when is it my turn to go on holiday? Nobody thinks about me. And your father, he is of no help either. When he is not at work, he is in the church. When he is home he wants to listen to his gramophone records. The entire Mattheüs Passion and then I am not allowed to say a single word. And you, you also do nothing for me. Being the Grand Lady there in Leyden, feasting and what not and leaving me here to work all day". Ma could easily continue this for hours, never repeating herself. She would save up all her grievances in order to ventilate them at a chosen opportunity.

It was impossible to satisfy Ma. When she was extensively feted at her birthday, the day after she would go to town to the warehouses such as *Bijenkorf* and *V&D* to see what all her presents had cost. Woe him or her if by accident you had spent below her norm! "Is that what I am worth to you? Not more? Oh, you had to do it on the cheap. It was only for your mother". Lotte never could escape this. Not even when she was married, being a mother herself: "No Gus, we have to buy something more. You came up with something really nice for her and she will be really very pleased with it. But it cost too little! Shall we add 20 red roses? Then it will be approximately right. Remember, she knows that you are a scientific officer at the University and that you have a nice salary. Therefore you can afford to spend more on a birthday present".

Pa ten Brink was a thinnish back-country little man. He was like a male spider, who had absolutely no say at home. He brought home the money that his wife and children subsequently spent. If and when there was not enough money, Pa would work extra hours and Ma went to the presbytery begging for money. Both techniques would work but the first one had the advantage that Pa then not needed to listen to the fulminations of his wife. Whom he steadfastly called "Mother"; he was the only one in this, since all the children called her "Ma". Perhaps there existed an Oedipus complex here; true or not, it typified the strange relations within this family.

Their marriage had remained childless for the first six years. In the end their family physician had sent them to a sexologist. Yes, believe it or not, these existed even in the early 20th century; you just had to find them. Medically speaking nothing was wrong; both partners were healthy and capable of reproduction. Pa was perhaps a little too shy and a whole lot too pious; perhaps he was influenced by the 'dirty' and sinful image of sex that the Church brandished at the time.

With Ma you would certainly not expect any such restraints. Not only did she despise everyone and everything in and around the RC Church. From her you would rather expect that she would enjoy sex but that she was frustrated by the lack of it. She was large with deep black hair. Her background was in the Breda region of North Brabant and the Spanish garrison there had left its marks during several centuries of occupation. Not only her black hair but also her fierce temperament had clear Spanish overtones. Not surprisingly, it also had been Ma who had spied E. in the parish choir and she had decided that he would do.

Now they were with the sexologist, who – with the aid of life-size dolls – showed Pa what the idea was. "Deep into it, sir, as deep as you can go and then let go. Don't hold it up. You must let yourself go completely". After this practical look-see-do instruction, Lotte was made, but Pa had never forgiven his oldest that she was born from this 'dirty' porno stuff. Later, Lotte had sought support with her father, crying about the problems between her and her mother. But he had brusquely sent her away, refusing to interfere and telling Lotte to solve her own problems with "Mother". He was not getting himself involved!

If, by now, you would begin to think that Pa was rather a coward, you would be very wrong. During the war, Pa had been one of those silent Resistance people, who had been involved with such life-threatening activities like manufacturing forged documents, smuggling hand guns and hide downed RAF airmen and bring them to safe places. More than enough to get himself instantly shot by the Germans should he ever get caught. Treason was everywhere and in spite of that danger he had gone ahead and risked his life, at the same time risking the welfare of his family. Now, what was this? Reckless heroism or pious insanity, because God would stand guard over his family and everything would turn out OK? In the meantime he had learned the trick in doing his duty as a husband. During those war years in particular it had its advantages to make more babies. That meant more milk coupons for Mother, but also extra coupons for coal to keep the home at least partly warmed. "Come on E.", Ma would say, "do it again". For her pleasure and for the coal. And in this way a large family came into being with seven children. Nicely balanced with the first three reflecting all the psychotic ailments of Ma, and the last three as normal as could be. In between the number four, androgynous by nature but rather harmless. She had mostly remained outside Ma' influence by staying in a nun's boarding school in Limburg from the age of twelve till about nineteen. First secondary education followed by teaching college. Not that she could escape from the nuns without mental damage.

"Take off that bra. The boys can see your shape!"

"No lacquered shoes. Because by reflection of the light the men might look under your skirt!"

How on earth did they dream up these things?

That Ma was really psychotic was a well-kept secret in the Ten Brink family. However, she had been taken into a psychiatric hospital ward several times. On one occasion she had overheard the word "psychotic" from a discussion between two medical doctors who were treating her. She had demanded to know what that word meant. But no one had dared to tell her, least of all her family members.

IV

Higher Calling, War and Sex

In the meantime I had become a man many times, before I really became a man. Primary school, well, that was something I simply had to get through and that without being an altar boy anymore. The only new excitements were with my other grandparents. As a result of us moving we now lived quite close to them. Not only my *oma* and *opa* – the parents of my father – lived there but in the same house lived also two unmarried daughters and on the ground floor lived uncle Lucien with his wife. My grandparents had bought and equipped a complete butchery for uncle Lucien, very modern with all the machinery needed. Uncle Lucien would buy at the slaughterhouse a complete cow or pig which he then reduced to eatable delicacies. There was very little he could not use; the horns, the hoofs and the hide and that could be sold to the hide merchant.

Once, on a free Wednesday afternoon, I was allowed to go with him to the slaughterhouse. A cow was selected and she was then driven into a yoke. A laborer had a kind of pistol that was put onto the forehead of the cow. When the trigger was activated a steel pin was driven into the cow's forehead. That was not fatal but it was sufficient to stun the animal. Its knees buckled and then came the critical moment. One of the butchers quickly stepped forward to cut the throat of the cow with a big knife. Blood began to gush in big waves into a waiting tub. The heart kept pumping until there was nothing left to pump. Not exactly a joyful sight and this little boy too began to turn green. Next there was a lot of hacking and sawing and finally the cow was loaded onto a truck, complete with pails and tubs with blood, intestines, stomachs, udders and what not, because all that could be converted into money. I much enjoyed making sausages, but also the headcheese, the liver paste, the scrapple and the brawn were master pieces of old-fashioned tradesmanship. The image that kept coming back, though, was that of the big knife and the gushing blood.

I again became a man when God rejected me. I had wanted to become a priest and very badly so. Now the day approached that secondary school was nearing. I wanted to go to the Junior Seminary but my mother had firmly opposed it. However, we all had undergone a psychological test and there it said in print that I was University material and that I should therefore go to the Gymnasium, a Grammar School with Latin and Greek just like he Junior Seminary. Why I wanted so desperately to become a priest? Because I had seen how powerful and mighty they were and how they received respect and prestige from just about everybody. They were also the only ones who were entitled to conduct Consecration during Mass and who could give the Sacraments. However, I also knew full well that God had to call you and I heard nothing from Him! I even went back to my old parish church, where much of the sculptures had been made by my *opa*. The same church where I had been baptized and where I had done my First Communion. I prayed with all the fiery intentions I was capable of: "Lord, please call me!" However, God remained silent and the Calling never came. This was a terrible letdown, a real flop and that before His Image. In tears I had to accept that He did not want me and that I had to become a man in some other way. Of course, God knew what he was doing; He had seen right through me. It would take many years before I would understand this myself.

OK, Gymnasium then, I thought, because if you finished that properly then you could immediately enter the Senior Seminary and with that little detour you could become a priest after all. My mother decided the issue in a different manner: "No way. That Gymnasium would make you far too uppity". Translation: becoming a priest was far too high on the social ladder compared to our present status. "Go to Teaching College; then you can become a school teacher, just like uncle Mister". That too was higher in prestige compared to my father's position, but for my mother that was as far as she could calculate the consequences. Uncle Mister I had never known personally, but I knew that he had been a legendary schoolmaster in our little town. He had been the school teacher in the one-room school of old. He was famous for his storytelling exploits. At school all children would listen open-mouthed, because indeed he was a great narrator. He could tell of other countries and the world as if he had been there himself.

In the *café* where *oma* stood as owner, he was a visitor who was always welcomed. When uncle Mister started telling his stories about the *Zouaves* who had fought to defend the Pope, everyone stayed longer and that meant extra drinks. Uncle Mister's wife happened to be my *Oma*'s sister and when uncle Mister died, it was only natural that great-aunt Sjaantje came to live with my *Oma* and *Opa*.

In the meantime I protested all I could and it ended in a compromise. I was allowed to go to the HBS, the *Hogere Burger School,* a 5-year High School of higher standing but without Greek or Latin. Its diplomas would give automatic access to Universities but not to all Faculties thereof. And, of course, also no direct access to the Senior Seminary.

In the meantime the armies raced through our area. Bombardments, paratroopers, Canadians, British and Americans. With sweets, corned beef and white bread that we had never seen before let alone tasted. We could very easily have been killed, in this violent war, but it did not happen, at least not to us. Strangely enough all this barely moved me. I had seen a lot of things and not just those marching and singing German troops. At a certain moment we saw the *Grüne Polizei* running through our back gardens, evidently looking for an escaped prisoner. They rang all doorbells and demanded to search our homes. This also with a neighboring housewife two houses removed. She happened to be from German descent and therefore greeted them in their home language while inviting them in for a cup of *ersatz* coffee. The coffee was served by her maid. However, what the gentlemen officers did not realize – and neither did we until shortly after the war – that was that the girl servant was a Jewish girl, who had been hiding there for years. Unbelievable levelmindedness by both women. I also encountered a German motor cyclist who was taking a rest. From his side car he was doling out all kinds of goodies such as sweets, underwear, shoes and canned food. He kept saying: *"Der Krieg ist vorbei"* (= the war is over).

Shortly before liberation I saw how a man was beaten up by a German soldier. This happened right in the street on an intersection. Presumably the man had given unsatisfactory directions to the German. German patrols, heavily armed with *Schmeisser* machine pistols and *Panzerfausten* (the German equivalent of bazookas) still went through the empty streets. Artillery shells whistled over our homes on their way to a target a few km away.

I was standing there for hours along that main motorway, watching the passing war materiel. First the withdrawing Germans, then a few days nothing and then finally our liberators. Still a few days later in our own street a horse cart appeared, pulled by collaborators, with young women with shorn heads on top who had consorted with German soldiers, now exposed and spitted upon by an angry population.

It became a chaotic winter with many sledge exploits to fetch wood from the forest so that our mother could cook her meals on the woodburning kitchen stove; gas or electricity were barely available or not at all. From the storage dump of shot-up army vehicles (we called it the auto cemetery) we stole shoes and whatever was left behind. Such as smoke grenades; they were great fun but they were dangerous too because you could easily lose a few fingers or worse. We experimented with rifle ammo in a vise. With a long nail and a hammer you could activate them. Of course with a little heap of sand on top because the cartridge would split open. When that trick was under control, we promoted to the much heavier .50 ammo. Even that went well; the bullet flew out but did not get very far, because the cartridge burst open dissipating the force of the explosion. In the end even the vise broke into pieces. We refrained from playing with complete tank grenades. Some boys in our neighborhood were more courageous. They would bang the grenade on the pavement until the shell itself got loose. They would carefully continue until they could pry the shell out of the cartridge and then some lovely play material would be available. Sometimes it was just black powder, good for interesting fires. With any luck the contents consisted of spaghetti-like cordite sticks. We would build a small airplane from cardboard, shoved a cordite stick into its tail end, lit it and *voilà* we had a rocket plane, just like the German *Messerschmidt* 262 fighter jets we saw occasionally in our skies.

We had endured several bombardments to our town and many artillery attacks. We survived, it was very exciting, but in truth it hardly moved me even though the chances were considerable that sooner or later we would get killed. Later I would learn the word "existentialism", but in fact that applied seamlessly to that time. It was not all those bombs and grenade shells, or about the black market, or he stealing of ammunition. I was sort of floating in a nothingness. Who was I? Where was I heading for? There was no school. However, we were prepared for the secondary school one cold morning a week with our overcoats on, in a small room belonging to the nunnery. Naturally all schools had been requisitioned by the military.

Suddenly it was all over and after a Summer that had seemed endless the normal life restored itself and then the HBS began.

As if it had been waiting for this moment, something else also started. Strange prickly hairs appeared on my underbelly. What were they doing there and why now, all of a sudden? My voice also changed but that happened to all boys. We knew that and therefore it was nothing to be ashamed of. However, about these strange hairs I learned nothing. Even my mother would not say anything except that it was normal. There it was again. Everything was normal the way it was and it was the way it should be. But you were never told why it ought to be that way and not some other way. Plenty of questions for a somewhat frightened little boy who did not know who he was. And who did not understand what was happening to him. Those hairs were not the most worrisome part even. That little peeing thing that normally just hung there also began to behave curiously. We had always been told that everything having to do with peeing was 'dirty' and sinful and that nobody should see it. You were also not allowed to touch it except when peeing of course, and you had to wear underpants even at night when wearing pajamas. And what was there so 'dirty' really? Horses and dogs also walked around nakedly and they were peeing whenever they liked it and they did not have to wear pants. Perhaps this too was part of that Great Secret? That little bungling thing suddenly became hard and thick and a whole bit longer. That disappeared usually but it also came back at the weirdest moments. And it got ever bigger, even four, five times longer than normal, fiery red and glowing hot. Godalmighty, that really hurt! It felt as if the whole thing was pulled out by a red-hot pair of tweezers while it went into a twitch. All you could do was to crouch down and wait until it passed. Usually it did just that but one day something else happened. The whole thing began to shake and throb and that hurt even more. As if knifes were cutting up my prick along the sides. However, even that passed and then you could relax. Matter of fact, then indeed a peaceful feeling came over your being. Again, I was becoming a man, but this time I understood it even less than on previous occasions.

V

Going Steady?

Softly I shoved my hand under her shawl until I found her hand so that I could put mine on top. And that was permitted! From that moment onward we were going steady, as it was called in those days. We had a 'relation', we were a couple for the world to see. The PD (= Place of Delict) was the Arena in Verona, Italy, where we were enjoying a performance of Verdi's opera Aïda. What was that? What on earth was I doing there? Running towards my misfortune perhaps? In any case I was running after my cock, because every time I saw this girl Lotte I got an immediate erection. High time to do something about that. Yes, God had seen it correctly. I had been endowed with a strong sexuality and I would never have been able to lead a celibate life. Now I was 24 years of age and still virgin. For the moment I did not think of that. Just holding her hand was enough to feel heavenly. Lots of water had flowed under the *Ponte Vecchio* before it got this far. I had fallen head over heels in love with this extraterrestrial being; unfortunately I had not gotten much response but also no rude rejection.

The Student padre had organized a touring car trip to Northern Italy, but a rat-poor student like me did not have the money for such a holiday. Lotte did, because she was already teaching part-time at some secondary school. Together with friend Karel, who was just as poor as I was, we had trekked through Europe, hitch-hiking all the way in order to arrive at the right moment at that convent in Venice where Lotte and her bus was supposed to be. We made it in the nick of time, after many adventures. We had gone to sleep under a high spruce tree on a thick pack of soft needles, only to wake up soaking wet at around 5 AM because it had started to rain during the night and even our friendly spruce could not withstand all that water. On another occasion we set up our pup tent a bit hastily in a meadow; we saw some cattle on the other side of the meadow, only to discover a little later that they were all young bulls. We also found out that you could hitch-hike almost anywhere except in the Alpine passes in Switzerland. So, like Hannibal, we crossed them on foot, shortcutting all these serpentines of the motorway. Perhaps none of that was very relevant except perhaps our meeting with a former SS officer in Southern Germany. He took us to his home where he ordered his wife to cook a meal for us (and us alone!), while he regaled us on stories why the SS was such an elite unit, voicing at the same time his conviction that all these stories about atrocities were pure lies, concocted to discredit the SS. Proudly he showed us his SS tattoos. We told him what we knew about the SS in the Netherlands. "All lies; never happened", was his constant reaction. We had to stay over and for once we slept again under bed sheets with a down cover. The next morning we got an excellent breakfast with two eggs, likely the only two eggs in the house. Was it relevant? It all formed part of another story, years later, when I undertook a pilgrimage to Santiago de Compostela.

However, they were not there at that convent guesthouse and we did not get in. Now, as most people know, in Venice very little grass grows and we could not find a spot to put up our little tent. Not knowing what else to do we tried it again at that convent. It was already after midnight and this time Brother Doorkeeper let us in after having demanded our passports and we were shown our beds. Naturally we fell asleep immediately, only to be awakened around 4 AM by a crowd of shouting students, demanding to know what the hell we were doing in their beds. Then the padre came by with our passports in his hands and we were allowed to stay and sleep some more.

The next morning I saw Lotte and the other girl-students and then we went out to explore the city. I immediately made a deep impression on Lotte by buying a white shawl for her. Be it from her own money, because I had none, but I haggled the price down to 30% of the original asking price. Walking through Venice we came upon the *Ponte del Sospiri*, the Bridge of Sighs. There we stood for a moment and I had sighed deeply and gripped her hand. A few days later we, the two intruders, were allowed to hitchhike with the students to Verona and from there the victory had started.

Back in Leyden this 'relation' was continued. However, now we have to explain a few things. I was 24 of age and this was only my first girlfriend? And Lotte 24 of age too and never had a boyfriend before. Never even had a date! How was that possible? Ah, those were the times, my friend. For myself I had gone out to try and make contacts with girls. A movie date, a dance, a fancy fair date, walked with a girl in a meadow to put a flower in her hair. Very romantic but that is as far as it ever got; just looking, no touching. The *mores* of the day held that I had still years of study ahead of me; as of now I had no prospects. And then there was the compulsory military service which would rob me of another two years. And then, there was still Maria. All women were Maria's and they all stood on a high pedestal. All girls had to be venerated as the mothers of our not yet sired children. Above all they needed to be protected. We men, we were supposed to protect them and certainly refrain from bringing them in problems, such as making them pregnant before the proper time. Therefore no touching because nothing was more shameful than making a girl pregnant so that a shot-gun marriage was required. This was still the time of before the Pill; condoms you could only get by becoming a member of the Netherlands Society for Sexual Reform and no Catholic in his right mind would ever do that. Those NSSR people, they were real perverts and notorious debauchees! We Catholic men, we were the courteous knights who in true admiration and veneration protected the women against all possible evil and supported and helped them wherever possible. And all that without asking anything in return. In true altruistic fashion, dedicated to Maria, the mother of Jesus, we Catholic young men stayed virgin until the wedding night; we did so out of idealism and full conviction. We knew that the Protestant boys said the same thing, but we also knew that they did it surreptitiously anyhow. As if God would not see it if you did it on the sly. I can bear witness that within our own group of Catholic students, which counted many 'couples' and even officially engaged pairs, no one did it. I would have known; these things never stay secret for any prolonged period of time.

But then that Lotte girl! She had managed to become 24 years of age without a single date, never a cup of coffee with anyone even. It took me years to understand this. Because Lotte - it bears repetition – looked really pretty and attractive. She was majoring in Mathematics and that was rather unusual for a girl. There were in any case few girls in the beta-sciences and those were mostly in Biology or Chemistry. Lotte had a (female) best friend from her own year called Elly, who was also in Math and this Elly was extremely popular with the boys. So Math was not the problem. In the end she told me that only once she had become infatuated with a boy, a certain Harry. That had been a long and fruitless longing, because Harry showed no interest in her. When Harry became engaged Lotte perhaps had thought: "Let me take this Gus, now that Harry is a lost case. He looks serious and I want something before I become a childless spinster". That puppy love for Harry might also explain why she never saw the yearning looks from all those boys around her. There was Leo, the biologist, who had taken her into his Executive just to be close to her. He waited and waited but never received the slightest encouragement. Why so hesitant, you dummy? Why did you not take action, by holding her hand, for example? That might have spared me untold misery and misfortune that undoubtedly would then have been poured over you. You have never known, man, what you have been spared. For years his hopeless love languished but eventually he had gotten married. I hope you are OK, Leo; believe me, it could have been worse.

There was another, alternative solution to the question why Lotte got so completely ignored by the young men. Ma had done her work very systematically and comprehensively, so that her oldest daughter was psychologically already entirely hung up and warped before she reached adulthood. Fact is she had Lotte saddled with a tremendous inferiority complex, where no love could ever penetrate anymore. Did these young men sense any of that, perhaps? However, now she had that oak tree that she could lean against and that chest she could cry on when another visit to her family had been so terrible again. At one time she had come back to Leyden totally in discomfort. Her mother had had one of her moments; not only had she complained again but this time she also had provided the remedy:

"I demand that you all love me. That I have earned for all my hard work".

"Oh, mother, if you demand it, then it becomes impossible. Love exists only if given voluntarily. Now that you demand it, I cannot give it anymore".

Lotte had cried because in this way she lost her mother. Ma did not relent, however. She stuck with her demand. In fact, Lotte had always loved her mother very much and now this love was taken away from her. That was the hinge point; from then on Lotte could not love anymore. Years later, during another visit to her parental home, Ma came back to the same point. The family sat at the table for a Sunday noon meal. All the children were present plus this one son-in-law plus already the first grandchild. Many reasons for a happy table but Ma had to spoil it again. However, this son-in-law was not to be cowered and contradicted her straight into her face so that everyone could hear it.

"I am entitled to your love", she said.

"No, Mrs. T, you are entirely wrong in that".

Suddenly a silence fell; a silence that could be heard. The clicking sounds of forks and knifes suddenly stopped and the table became a *tableau vivant* of dead people. Everybody looked with scared expressions direction Ma. Somebody had contradicted Ma. That never happened; nobody would dare. Not the children and certainly not her drone-husband. Ma looked frightful and she said:

"Are you not going to demand that from our own children when you have looked after them all their lives?"

"No, Mrs. T, I will certainly not do that. I will hope that they will love me, but if they don't, I will be sad but I will certainly not demand anything from them. Because love is unconditional. And it can only be given totally of free will. As soon as you demand it, then it becomes impossible to obtain it".

Prophetic words, but that I did not realize at that moment.

VI

Creaking Marriage

"Mieke , if your grades don't improve then I don't love you anymore".

We are some 25 years later and Mieke is our third daughter. The marriage is holding up, but don't ask how. Many tears later it is now Lotte who is guilty of gross shortcomings in the giving-of-love department. The same conditional love she had suffered so much from under Ma's regime, she is now perpetrating on her own children. The subject matter were Mieke's rather unimpressive results in her first University year. For myself I was not too concerned. Being a University professor I had seen enough students who still had to find their way. I knew that Mieke was very intelligent and that she had special gifts. I had a saying that I often used with concerned parents: "Talents always will come floating up". That is exactly what happened to Mieke too. She has found her way in life, but now she was being torpedoed by her own mother. This became the first time (and also the last) that I openly criticized my wife in the presence of a child:

"I love Mieke, whatever she does and she may count on that."

"So, do you find it normal, these results?"

"No, not at all; I regret these results as much as you do, but what I mean to say is that even now she may count on my support. It is cruel if you now belittle her and deny her your love. It is clear that Mieke has to go a different pathway than the one you designed for her. Which way that is I don't know at this moment but I would gladly discuss that with Mieke."

"She bloody well shall do what we tell her. Her two older sisters have shown the right example. If she refuses to do that, I will take my hands off her."

Later, when we were with ourselves again, I reproached Lotte that what she had just done to Mieke was exactly what she, Lotte, had suffered so much from, in the hands of Ma.

"Have you then forgotten that you asked me, no, begged me, to make sure that you would never become like Ma? At that time I promised you that if you ever would become that way I would put you over my knee and spank you on your bare bottom." She had then answered: "Can you really promise me that?" "I replied 'yes', and you seemed happy with my answer. Do you remember?"

"That was then and this is now. If you ever touch me I will call the police." Just to make sure I asked Lotte:

"What would you do if one of your two eldest committed a murder?"

"Then she is no longer my child".

Those two daughters had always performed to expectations, hèr expectations. Always the first at school and forever they had won all possible prizes. Now, immediately the villainous, rejecting, unfeeling, loveless judgement. Even these two, so highly favored by their mother at the present, could never count on her unconditional love. Their entire lives they would have to slave on a daily base to keep fulfilling the high expectations of this new "Ma".

My reply to Lotte was simple. Of course, murder is a terrible thing, but they were my children and when they might end up in jail, they would need help. I would not condone any crime, but I would stand by them and help where I could. Perhaps only by being there, in their moment of need and loneliness. Lotte would have nothing of that. In her mind children who would insult her by such behavior would not be entitled to her love. There was that expression again; entitlement to love. I just left, torn and with bad premonitions. She did not love me, that was well-known and obvious. Just as clearly she did not love her children. Then whom did she love? Did she love herself or did she perhaps despise herself whenever she looked in the mirror? She was sufficiently intelligent to be capable of a certain degree of self-reflection, at least in the early years. On those occasions she saw sharply what was wrong with Ma, enough to fear that she might become just like her. Had I perhaps reacted the wrong way? In the past and now again? Perhaps I should have taken her pants down and given her a spanking on her bare bottom. Was she taunting me? Begging to be beaten? I would never know; fact is that I simply could not do it, not then in any case. And not later, not ever.

Our third daughter had rebelled, though, as Nos 3 quite often do. She quite explicitly indicated that she did not wish to follow the example of her two older sisters. She wanted to go her own way even as she did not know precisely what that route was. And she was prepared to accept the consequences. She did not need a fat pay cheque every month. A little modest home with a little envelope with some cash at the end of the week enough for a modest life style, that was enough for her. She did not want a University degree and therefore she had produced poor results so that she could get away from it.

VII

My Romantic Soul

When I look back it is especially looking back to my illusions. It had started all so innocently. So pure and so full of beautiful ideals. At the HBS I had gotten in contact with the Dutch literature and we had started with the *Carel ende Elegast* epic poem from the early Middle Ages. I read the piece so many times that it almost self-destructed. Courtly knights who tried to impress beautiful noble women; to love them also but only from a distance with a cloud of holiness around it all. My Dutch Language teacher became my counsellor. This was the time I began to write in earnest and soon enough I scored the highest marks for my stories. Of course, these never dealt with beautiful women; that I was not really allowed. However, I let blood-red suns slowly sink into the horizon, while robins sang their love songs, with their silhouettes profiled against the darkening sky while the poplars softly whispered. And then I would get an "A" again for this essay. The Flemish poet Guido Gezelle was also on the literature program and I was soon totally taken by his alliterative poetry. Jan Engelsman's epic poem "And the farmer he went on plowing" I could declaim by heart with great pathos.

Not to forget of course poets such as Willem Kloos with his: "I am a God in my deepest self". The latter I did not understand at all but it sounded great. The non-understanding undoubtedly was my fault; again a piece of mystique that I still had to grasp, some day. Here were all the examples for my life. My still empty Burgundian romantic soul now filled itself with the sweet rich wine from the land of Duke Jan. It also became a period of intense religiosity. True, I would never become a priest but my Savior was still the center of my life. In spite of the violent erections I was enduring almost daily I desired to lead a saintly life, be it preferably with a beloved woman at my side. After all, the very holy St. Brigitta had eleven children, hadn't she? With regularity my hormones became active at the sight of a well-filled blouse. My mentor said that this was OK. "Whenever it comes up, just pray a few Hail Mary's", he advised. Believe it or not, praying did help. Apart from masturbating it was the only thing that really made these erections disappear. Masturbating was a capital sin so in view of all things holy that also had to be avoided. "Hail Mary, full of grace".

Somewhere around this time we received "Sex Education". With our entire group of the HBS final year we went to a retreat where everything would be told. Indeed this was the straight truth. A medical doctor told us boys that those erections had a purpose. This penis was not just for peeing! The good doctor showed on the screen what girls and women looked like! And that is where the penis is supposed to go into, said the doctor. That is where all the stuff had to go into, and with that ejaculation went the little seeds that … blah, blah, blah. Hurrah, now we finally knew for sure. Finally no more backhanded hints or weird stories. Finally we all had become men, now that we were made responsible for the reproduction of the genus man.

After this medical story everything was spoiled immediately, however, by a Redemptorist priest, who told us that every erection was a sin and that in Confession we had to tell it. From that moment onwards I never have gone to Confession again, at least not for half a century. How could I explain that no day would pass without several moments of erection and what I did to combat it? This struggle lasted for at least ten years. In the end I gave up and said to the Lord: "Dear God, forgive me. You made me with this devil inside me. I am now going to give in. Because then at least I can sleep so that tomorrow I can get up early and be ready to work on my future. That girl Lotte that you sent onto my path, I love her dearly, but first I will have to do that doctoral exam. Therefore forgive me, my Lord, but it gives me indeed the rest and relaxation I need. After that I will be ready again to do Your Will."

VIII

Full Professor

The first time that Lotte let herself go against me, and I mean indeed AGAINST me, was the moment I came home with good news. I told her that at the University a proposal was in the works to make me a Full Professor. I had arrived in Canada with a tenured appointment as Associate Professor. Now, barely four years later, with me still not even 40 years of age, there was that proposal to make me a Full Professor, something that filled me with proud feelings. Yet another hinge point in the process of becoming a man, of becoming an adult, reaching top rank at a rather early age. However, rather than sharing my pride and joy on this day there followed a terrible explosion of resentment from Lotte's part.

"And when will I be promoted to Full Professor? Nobody thinks about me!"

"You are forgetting that you are a Sessional Instructor and that you are teaching Math to freshmen students".

"I have just as much right to a Full Professorate and they should just give it to me. No, the whole world is a conspiracy of all men against all women. And you in particular; you are one of those Male Chauvinist Pigs who are destroying my life".

She went on like this for hours with short breaks only to then start again. Was it indeed for hours or was it for weeks, or years of constant accusations? Impossible to reconstruct.

How I had ended up there in Canada? Ah, that had to do with my religion, with my being a Brabanter and with "Ma". That may sound unbelievable. That even defies anyone's imagination, although it was absolutely true.

First I had to learn more about the phenomenon Woman. True, I admired all women. I thought they were splendid, very special and certainly superior to us, poor men. We served mostly as mindless hulks, doing something terribly banal like making money, in order to purchase food and shelter, so that we could entice a female to come in. A female to have sex with, indeed something we enjoyed tremendously. However, our overall performance was less than brilliant. All we did was waging wars in which we killed each other by the millions plus each other's wives and children. Being now accused of exploiter of women was something totally at odds with my own life experience, my own philosophy and certainly contrary to my deeply felt love for this Lotte woman, who was mine. I just barely refrained from worshipping her, but I adored her in the finest Maria tradition. She was the mother of my children, she was my Princess, my little Queen. I always was thinking about her and never about other women. In principle and in daily fact she was my Everything.

IX

My Opa

Where had I gone wrong? My Dutch Language teacher had carefully imprinted me. My Religion teacher had put some sugar coating on top. And then there was my *Opa*. Remember, he was living on the first floor above the butchery of his youngest son Lucien. As his grandson I loved my *Opa* very much; I admired him for many reasons. For example, he was the only one who could tame the guard dog Duuk. With such a butchery you needed a guard dog. If not, you could reckon on being burglarized by persons who wanted access to all these delicacies. *Opa* just chased Duuk into his dog house and then proceeded to clean the pen. Duuk just lay there grunting with bared teeth but he never attacked *Opa*. Any other person he would have bitten in the buttocks. Small wonder that this grandson admired his *Opa* immensely. *Opa*'s garden was another thing. Nowhere else the dahlias flowered so richly. His secret? In a butchery there is always lots of waste materials; not all blood may be transformed into sausage. Then *Opa* would dig a hole somewhere to get rid of that waste. Then some soil on top and next year the marigolds would flower there abundantly. And also the broad beans, the green beans, not to forget the string beans and the sweet beets. Nothing of organic nature was thrown out. And when we were done and everything had been raked properly and neatly, he would unbutton his trousers and urinate over it all. Naturally I joined him in this effort. However, my thin little trickle was nothing compared with the enormous waterfall he unleashed over the spinach. There came no end to it; that man must have had a gallon-sized bladder. As soon as he had finished he let go of a tremendous fart, that resonated between the neighboring houses. "OK", he then said with an extremely satisfied, almost angelical expression on his face: "Much better into the wide, wide world than in a narrow hole". Or he admitted to me with a stern face, even before he buttoned up his trousers: "When the water level drops, the ice will crack." At home, that is to say in his own home, he was not allowed to say such things. His wife Irene and his daughters Sientje and Sjaantje constantly scolded him and then chased him out. My *Opa* was indeed an earthy man. He taught me to always put my bare hands into the soil and to never wear garden gloves. "You have to feel the soil, the grains and the fatty texture with your fingers and then you should actually also taste it", he would say and he then proceeded to give the right example. What I did not realize at such a moment, that was that these same hands had been very creative.

Opa was usually not allowed to eat at the table with the others because he slurped. He had one of those antique *moustache* cups with a porcelain bridge across so that his enormous moustache would not hang in his soup. He had to eat at the counter and then was chased out. He was extremely proud of his moustache. The last bulwark of his manliness, you might say. He was only barely tolerated and that only because he brought in a substantial pension on a weekly basis. Being a sculptor he had been afflicted with the shaking sickness and his oldest daughter had then found a job for him at the Tungsten light bulb factory. Not that this would do him any good. He was forced to surrender his pay (and later his pension) at home. As concession they would then give him 75 cent a week so that he could buy his pipe tobacco.

"You see, my little boy, you have to be careful and watch out all the time. Never just try anything. Before you know it, little babies are on their way and then you are forever stuck." He knew. That is how he himself had gotten stuck. Just like the other tradesmen he had slept on the straw in the attic above the inn opposite the church. In that church there was plenty of work for my *Opa* because a good sculptor he was. As long as there was work he could not leave. Only after all the work was completed the tradesmen were paid for the last time and then they would be on the road again. In this manner *Opa* had travelled through half of Europe: the Rhineland, Belgium, Southern Netherlands and North-East France. Sometimes he told me bits of that past, especially when I told him that again lots of German words were creeping into his speech. After 10-12 years of hay stacks, country inns and fast loves he had arrived in our town, where he not only found lots of work but also a desirable inn keeper's daughter. Then he had committed a stupid mistake. He had not only made this daughter pregnant, but he had done so while there was still plenty of work: "You see, my son, I could not run off, because then I would never have found work anywhere. No master sculptor will take you on once you have run off while there was still work to do. That is the law of the road. First finish your work and then you may go."

They got him and they did not let go of him. Shortly before the nineteen's century ended he and his bride Irene were married in the same church that he was still beautifying.

However, compared to that, Lotte and I had done it much better. We had stayed away from each other's body, we had finished our studies, we had found jobs and were squirrelling away money to buy a home and furnishings. Was it really that much better? Indeed, there was a lot of idealism behind it and it had required a lot of will power. On the other hand there were also substantial disadvantages to our way of having a relation. If only we had lived ten years later! Undoubtedly we would then have used the Pill and we would have shacked up even before having completed or studies just like everybody did ten years later. The time that the pill arrived was also the time of the Beatles, of the hippies, of free love, of white (i.e. free) bicycles and of much more. The whole idealistic frame work had collapsed as a house of cards; undoubtedly Lotte and I would have joined in. Then I could have given in to my very urgent urges and next I would never have married Lotte. I would not have felt obliged to do anything and neither would she have. We both would have played house with each other and in the end we would have gone different ways to build and complete our lives in a different way. And all that with considerably less problems. Fewer tears would have been shed; less blood (real or virtual) would have flowed.

In the meantime, on a Saturday afternoon, when I was working in *Opa*'s garden, he came running from the house. Actually, he could not really run, because he was well into his eighties, but even so his wooden shoes came in rapid tempo in front of his body. That was just as well since otherwise he would surely have fallen on his nose. I did not even look at his feet; all I saw was that frightened expression in those soft big brown eyes that I knew so well. Eyes that now looked wild, as wild as his snorting nose. *Mon Dieu,* what had happened? A bit later he could tell it, be it in mixed-up order and stunted sentences. I understood that they had wanted to shave off his moustache! With "they" he meant the three women. Together they had concocted a weird plan. They wanted to celebrate his Golden marriage jubilee and for that purpose he was to look smart and therefore that dirty moustache had to go. But he was not going to collaborate with that plan. He had been scared almost out of his wits but soon enough he had his senses back. He had told them that indeed he was getting old, not senile and that he still could count. He knew therefore that the Golden marriage jubilee was next year, not this year. He was not going to play with the little game to promote aunt Sientje from a 3-month baby to a 15-month baby. "Ridiculous", he snorted and that was about as strongly as he was going to express himself. He had too much inner civilization to utter his indignation more vehemently.

However, his moustache stayed! In the end that 49 year marriage jubilee was indeed celebrated; the neighborhood accepted it without a murmur. The parish priest also accepted it. For an extra fl.100,- banknote he would gladly let the marriage license booklet closed and unseen. In addition a Holy Mass with three celebrants also brought extra revenue. The entire *hocus pocus* was rather innocent anyway, like a crime without a victim. So, *Opa* got a new suit with a coordinated dress shirt, a new tie and new shoes. The latter pinched his toes, but that was all. He let it all happen to him, knowing that it was in fact all paid for by his own money. His proud moustache had stayed and that counted. It had been trimmed a bit but in his new outfit he looked proud. To me he whispered: "What a monkey business, hè?" Again that undercooled attitude. It was much like a puppet show and it was below his dignity to get wound up about it.

My *Opa* would not live that long after that. We all thought he would die of lung cancer, because he was a life-long smoker. When he worked in his garden in the hot sun, he would often take off his undershirt and then you could see something truly amazing. On his chest you would see his lungs outlined in yellowish brown. Nicotine and tobacco tar had penetrated his flesh and in fact perforated his skin so that they came to the surface of his outer skin. No, it was not lung cancer that killed him. In the end he died from arteriosclerosis of the brains. That resulted in some anxious moments, because he became delirious and all kinds of stories came to the fore, including some that the family would rather not have heard. Again he trusted his grandson, now sixteen years old, much more than the rest and so he told me that he was a murderer! His story was very confused, in bits and pieces and much of it in German, the language that now was again very prominent with him. There had been a row in an inn, now some seventy-odd years ago. Of course it had been all about the favors of a local maiden. At a certain moment my *Opa* had become so angry that he had pulled a knife and had plunged it into his rival's chest. Lots of blood had flowed, he told me, gasping, lots of blood everywhere. He had jumped up from his seat, ran out and kept running for three days, until he felt safe from pursuing *Feldwebels*. At that time, the police forces were not that organized and so he had escaped. He had never been caught, but now he wondered whether the other had indeed died, or that he perhaps had survived. It was impossible to ever answer that question and so my grandfather went into the hereafter, knowing that quite possibly he was a murderer. For me it did not matter at all. I thought that he looked splendidly there in his coffin. I was tremendously proud of him. His big nose stood proudly straight up in the air and that moustache lay around his mouth. Pity he never could see himself this way.

X

Murder?

"I will kill you", Lotte screamed.

It was about 3 AM and – as was more or less customary these years - , Lotte had punched me awake because she wanted to talk as she said, but in fact it was always to scold and insult me verbally. She got up and ran downstairs. At that time we had a wooden home and therefore you could always hear where somebody was going. From the bedroom through a short corridor, eight steps down to the living room, turn right to the upper foyer, down six steps more down to the lower foyer, another little corridor to the left and then you were in the kitchen, in fact straight below our bedroom.

I heard how she opened one of the drawers followed by the metallic sound of cutlery. I heard her coming up the stairs again, then she sat down on the highest step. I could not see her, but I heard every move she made. After a while she got up and went down again. Then again that drawer and the sound of cutlery. Finally she returned to the bedroom, silently stepped into the bed, turned away and proceeded to sleep.

The next morning I went immediately to the kitchen, even before Lotte was up. No, not to make tea this time; rather to pull open that drawer and there on top of all the table knifes, the boning knife lay diagonally across. That boning knife we used only rarely; now it lay across the other knifes on top. In her sick mind Lotte had discovered the perfect murder weapon. A solid, curved handle of layered black and white hard plastic that allowed a good grip. Then a short blade of perhaps only three inches length, ending in a point. You did not have to be strong. Just place the point between the ribs and push; without much force needed, the heart would be perforated. The same point against the carotid artery and even less pressure would be needed to produce a fatal wound. Yes, Lotte had thought about all this, that is for sure.

XI

Brabant and the Brabanter

We are now getting ahead of ourselves. The distance from Duke Jan of Brabant to the 4th Balkenende cabinet in the 21st century is dizzying. First Brabant would be denigrated again and again; all that would create the Brabant soul and would in fact ennoble it. A soul which in the 20th century would become a near-extinct entity. Perhaps she is already extinct. All this we have to understand if we want to understand the absurdist love/hate story between Lotte and Gus. How on earth came Lotte to wanting to kill her husband, a man filled with noble ideals who had done everything in his power to make her happy. Who had – in the process – often neglected his own needs and wishes.

One second of inattention had cost Duke Jan his life. He was a superstar in the art of horse riding and of the jousting games where oncoming opponents were made to bite the sand. They used lances with heavy leather-covered ends so that they would not really harm each other. While Duke Jan conquered more and more territory, the jousting games were also practiced wherever he appeared. Naturally under the admiring eyes of many lovely ladies.

There the knights galloped towards each other, in harness and helmets, the visors closed and the lances high. At the right moment these lances would be lowered in an attempt to unseat the opponent. Unfortunately Jan, the winner in so many tournaments, had made a little miscalculation and now he lay in the grass, not just humbled but severely wounded. A few days later he died in hellish pains. A pity, because in his short life he had cobbled together quite a nice little empire. He had brought Peace and Justice and in particular the Fine Arts had blossomed and now this whole Burgundian area flourished as never before. Much of that survived after the untimely death of Duke Jan. In this land the people had certain characteristics in common, a joint understanding of what is beautiful or good and what isn't. During the next reigns of Dukes, Lords and Kings those characteristics were allowed to develop, most visibly so in the Fine Arts.

At school we learnt that the 17th century was our Golden Century, the century of the famous Dutch School of painters like Rembrandt, Vermeer and the like. The same history books barely mentioned the other Golden Centuries, much earlier, in the 13th, 14th, and 15th century. Those golden days lasted much longer, flourished more substantially and actually paved the way for Rembrandt and his cohorts. This golden time, together with Duke Jan and his influence were dealt with in two or three pages in our History books. The much later 17th century Golden Century is extensively treated in those same History school text books. What is this? Some kind of willful falsification of history, that is what it is. The remarkable thing is, that if you lived in Southern Catholic Netherlands, in North Brabant say, you would get to hear, read and be taught the same nonsense, even in all the Catholic schools. Stranger yet, those History school texts in the Catholic schools all had the *nihil obstat* (= no objection) or *Imprimatur* (= may be printed) seal of approval from the bishops! What moved the bishops to not only condone but actually collaborate in this deliberate rewriting of History? We found only a single History school booklet, this one for primary school use and written for Roman Catholic schools (titled "Red White Blue") that explicitly stated in the foreword and also in the main text that it wanted to highlight this "from the South arriving civilization". Curiously, this is the only History school text, written for Roman Catholic schools that bears no approval from the bishop. In the same vein, why on earth decided the bishops that the first Catholic University should not be created in the Southern provinces? Nijmegen, just outside the Catholic region was selected for that purpose. Perhaps my *Opa* would have known the reason. He once told me: "Never rile up those Gents above the Great Rivers. Just say Yes, sir, and keep your head down." And pay taxes, of course. In Brabant people considered 'Holland' a kind of pestilence, something to shy away from, if possible. As the saying went, you were advised not to stir up the shit so that you were then perhaps just ignored. This attitude bespeaks a kind of subservience, a kind of gentle slyness. It certainly had to do with centuries of suppression and discrimination. Was perhaps in this way the soft Brabant character molded or was it the other way around?

The Reformation had come with unheard-of cruelties. In the name of freedom of religion all religions were forbidden except that of the Dutch Reformed Church. How that could be reconciled with God's word and Jesus' teachings of love, is a total mystery to me. And how it could be explained in terms of logic, that I would like to see explained to me. All priests, nuns and friars had to leave the towns and in fact the country under threat of death. In long files these human processions moved from North to South. Not only the Catholic way of worshipping was outlawed but also the care for the poor, the sick, the widows and orphans and the old people was abruptly ended because the usual caregivers such as the nuns and friars were also banned. All Church property was confiscated and declared property of the State or of the town or of the Reformed Church. This was of course organized theft which in character and method was no different from the way Jewish property was stolen by the Nazis in World War II. The comparison is appropriate because the same techniques were used. It is rumored that Hitler's Plenipotentiary Seyss Inquart laughed himself into a stupor when he was told how the Dutch Reformed Church had done it. You make a little pseudo law (never mind that it was not lawful) to provide the appearance of lawful action. Often the members of the church communities were forced to become protestant. How could they have done differently if you first remove their spiritual leaders? From these new-protestants was next asked to declare that they had changed over together with all property to the new religion. A document was then drawn up to 'legalize' the conversion. It was then overlooked that these people had no legal right to do so, since all churches, land and other property were not theirs; these were owned by the Catholic Church, the Diocese in particular. The Dioceses were the true owners and they are still that today. Nowadays property stolen from the Jews is still being returned to these owners or their heirs. This includes goods handed over under coercion or forcibly sold at prices under the market value. When will the State of the Netherlands and the Dutch Reformed Church return those stolen properties to their rightful owners? When will Brabant and the Brabanters receive an official apology from the State and from the Reformed Church? Brabant became a 'Generality' land. Do you know what that meant? Amongst others, its inhabitants barely had any legal personality. They had no voting rights, neither passive nor active, therefore no representation in the Government. Subjects they were; barely anything more than slaves. Requests for Province status were denied time and again. Ah, yes, they were allowed to pay taxes; against the same rates as in rich Holland. A farmer in Holland could easily put twelve cows on a hectare of his clay-rich meadows; in large portions of Brabant only one cow could barely find sustenance on one hectare of his sorrel-infested marshland. However, that Brabant farmer paid just as much taxes for his hectare as did a Holland farmer. Until well into the 20th century all his cash went to taxes. That one cow produced milk; not for the farmer's children but rather for the communal milk factory where it was converted to butter; the money for this butter was the only cash basis for paying the taxman. Exploitation, extortion, much worse than in the colonial areas. Show your indignation you politically-correct thinking Hollander;

wake up Brabanter, you with your kind indulgence. For centuries you let yourself be trodden upon.

The first bridge across the Great Rivers was finished in 1869. That was the rail bridge across the river Waal near Culemburg, South of Utrecht, quickly followed by similar bridges near Zaltbommel and Hedel. In this way the rail connection Amsterdam-Utrecht-'s-Hertogenbosch-Eindhoven was realized. Shortly after that, in 1871, the mile-long Moerdijk bridge was finished so that Rotterdam too got its connection with the South. Not meaning to dirt-poor Brabant but rather to connect to Brussels and Paris. These were all rail bridges, built, not to serve passengers but rather to foster trade and commerce. Not to open up Brabant; no, that area was supposed to remain a marshy backwater intended as a barrier against potential French invaders. For that reason the infrastructure of Brabant was deliberately neglected. Those Brabanters should continue their farming; then they remained non-dangerous. All well-paying positions were reserved for Protestant persons. That went very far. A municipal horse dung collector, who went around in the streets with a little cart to collect and remove the horse manure had to be a practicing member of the Dutch Reformed Church. Why? Simply because this was a position in the civil service and all civil servants had to be Protestant. Around 1910 this was still the general situation. Did you never wonder what the father of Vincent was Gogh was doing as a Protestant clergyman in 100% Catholic towns like Zundert and Nuenen? That too was simple. Naturally the town mayor was Protestant and so was the town's Secretary. If there was a (one-room) school then of course the school teacher was also Protestant. And therefore a small Protestant church building had to be provided plus a minister of the cloth. That is why in that Catholic Brabant you may still find these tiny Protestant church buildings.

Slowly, very slowly, improvements did manifest themselves. The emancipation of the Catholics in the Netherlands got to a start in 1853, when a Concord with the Vatican was concluded. Roman Catholicism was no longer a forbidden religion, bishops and priests were allowed back and churches could be built. It was called the Restoration of the Ecclesiastical Hierarchy. North Brabant had become a real Province of the Netherlands, thanks to the French revolution. "Ha, Generality lands, that means it does not belong to anyone", the French revolutionaries had thought, "so we will annex it". And right away French Republican troops had marched into North Brabant. In The Hague politicians woke up and immediately awarded North Brabant (and also Drenthe, another Generality land) Provincial status. When it became clear that there was no danger for Drenthe to be lost, its new Provincial status was again withdrawn.

The French occupation under Napoléon Bonaparte had not brought much relief for Brabant either. The good King Louis Napoléon had been appointed by his brother as *Roi d'Hollande* and pointedly not as *Roi des Pays Bas*. Brabant just became part of France and was allowed to provide thousands of its young men as cannon fodder. However, Napoléon had been defeated and by the subsequent Peace Treaty of Vienna in 1815 Prince William VI of Orange had been appointed to rule as King Willem I over a United

Greater Netherlands. That included, apart from the present Netherlands, also Belgium and Luxembourg. Picardy, a Dutch speaking area in North West France, once conquered by King Philippe of France he did not get back. The new King overplayed his hand quite ruinously. He too, guided by his Hollander advisors kept on discriminating the South, still forbidding their religion and of course advantaging the Holland cities in all trading matters. His son, the later King Willem II understood far better these matters, but he was unable to ward off the disaster that his father was creating. In 1830, after a short civil war, the most Southerly part split off to continue as the State of Belgium. In 1839 the division became official. Poor Brabant was cut in two, quite literally. The Northern half with all those lovely marshes continued as the Province of North Brabant in the State the Netherlands.

Towards the end of the 19th century special (meaning Catholic) education became legalized. The Brabanters obtained passive and active voting rights and a Catholic political party was founded. Yes, indeed, the Brabanter appeared to become a real human being. After two and a half century of suppression those old sentiments died out only very slowly, however. *De facto* discrimination persisted for a very long time. Up to and including Queen Wilhelmina we had monarchs who were rather violently anti-Catholic. Many professions and public offices remained closed off for Catholics. We personally would experience it more than a century after that hinge point of 1853. However, the Resurrection of the Brabanter, once started, was unstoppable.

XII

Great-Grandfather, Grandfather, Father

And so it happened that my great-grandfather emigrated North from the depths of deep-Belgium. That happened in 1870 but it had nothing to do with the Franco-Prussian war that was waged in that year. My grandfather-to-be was just one year old at the time. My great-grandfather had taken a look at his rather numerous offspring and had decided that the grass was greener there up North. That was indeed well-considered, because he had been trained as a sculptor in the School of Ghent and up North plenty new churches were being built. That was legal once more, but sculptors they did not have there. No, in that barbarous land they were only very good in hacking sculptures to pieces. However, now was the time for a catching-up. Great-grandfather had imprinted on his sons that life as a sculptor is pretty rotten at best so that they should not follow his example. However, his youngest son ignored that advice and he learned that trade in the School and atelier of the Brothers Cuypers, where great-grandfather had found work. Yes, indeed the Brothers Cuypers; the one ran this sculpting School and the other made fame as an architect, designing in Amsterdam the Central Railway

Station and the *Rijksmuseum* of Fine Arts. He had also designed the parish church where my grandfather had worked so intensively on. The same Cuypers who had also designed the chapel of the Sisters of Love where I had been altar boy, the very chapel that I had loved so much.

Somewhat against his plans my grandfather had gotten stuck in a Brabantine environment. However, it could have been much worse. His wife Irene soon became the owner of that *café* across from the church and she soon showed herself to be a very able publican. She would take her customers by the throat and threw them out, after having checked their pockets, of course, for any loose coins. Business is business and as a business woman she was not the lesser to any man. My *Opa* actually was not so badly off either. At least he could get rid of his seed in regular fashion and frequency. Many babies were sired, about half of them survived. He was an able tradesman although no Master. However, among the tradesmen he was the *figurist*, the one who did the faces and the hands. "Those hands, Gus, are even more difficult than the face", he told me once. Others did just flowers, or clothing; faces and especially hands that was something quite different. Then the Master of the atelier would come by, would nod his approval and then the sculpture went away under the name of the Master. My *Opa* never minded that. He never consider himself an artist. "Crazy modern ideas", he would say while shaking his head. When the stone dust created silicosis in his lungs, he shifted to wood and there he flourished even more. In those days sculptors died young; many died of silicosis and in the end the 'shaking' disease finished the career of my *Opa*. The constant hammering caused problems much like the tennis arm or the mouse arm in modern times. Carpal dysfunction is the official name of this chronic infection of the protective fleece around the nerves.

He had much disliked his degradation to factory worker. However, his wife had told him that she had no patience with freeloaders and that he had to make money somehow. His dignity was in question now and I guess that this was the moment that he began to hate his wife. By the time I got to know this *Oma* and *Opa* couple, there was evidently no love or even affection anymore between them. They still slept in the rather narrow conjugal bed of old; for unclear reason this could not be changed, apparently. But mutual affection? No, only a deep disgust from her part for this no-good, whom she steadfastly addressed with: "Hey, you". From his side a silent, wounded, not comprehending sadness, that actually you could not call "hate". If only he had really hated her! If only he would have stood up to her! No, for that he was too sweet, too soft, too civilized.

In that environment my father had been born together with his siblings. In a material sense they were doing OK; they had leather shoes and therefore they did not have to go to the "wooden shoe school" of the poor. My father was even allowed a little bit of extra education beyond the compulsory six years of primary school. Later he took some courses in bookkeeping. In his free time he sometimes climbed in a pear tree and then he whistled a few tunes on his piccolo. On the opposite side of the block this was noticed by the Doreleyers girls, who wondered for whom these sweet serenades really were meant. Yes, that block. That was a micro cosmos in its own right, with its own history going back for centuries.

XIII

Willibrord and Later

Centuries ago, when St. Willibrord had come by on his travels, he discovered to his surprise that there was already a Christian community. The Romans had arrived in our little hamlet well before him. That was about the year 300 AD; our place in the woods near a couple of brooks had been put on a Roman map. Together with the soldiers all kind of other folks had trailed along such as a Christian teacher who wanted to convert these pagans. These Frankish hunters-farmers liked what they heard and in fact a little church was built. On the land of the absentee owner, the Emperor of Rome. Willibrord had seen to it that some land was officially given for the church and for agriculture and in addition some more land for the nuns to build a convent also with extra land for agricultural purposes, so that they could take care of their own needs for shelter and food. Around it a small village nucleus arose which yet later developed into our little town and a little farther on a real city. That is why I say sometimes that I have been a Catholic for some 1500 years; I mean with it that Jesus' teachings of love had arrived and developed in my place already fifteen centuries ago. That Brabantine characteristic of indulgence probably was not caused by the Protestant suppression, certainly not exclusively, but had rather found its base and was developed in the Burgundian Christianity, grafted on the Frank genes of softness. We Brabanters were the descendants of these early Frank tribes who in a wide arch turned away from the Great Rivers, Southward, here and there founding small communities. We should have stayed together and should not have mixed genes with other peoples. We were good and wholesome in ourselves, with our brown eyes, dark hair and certainly our moustaches, with our fertile seed and above all with our strong belief in a God who in the end always proved to be a loving and understanding Father, even when in the meantime you starved to death from lack of food or simply died from one pestilence or another.

The Clarisse nuns owned way too much land. Already for a long time they did not need any land anymore, because they were loaded and could buy anything they needed. They did not have to work because you did not get in unless you brought with you a whole lot of money. Afterwards you never got out again, except to vote for the Catholic State Party or horizontally, to be buried in the cemetery. They were a contemplative Order; all they did was praying, all day long, every day, to make up for those people who did not pray enough. In the end most of their land was sold to the Municipality, who promptly built a street through it to complete the fourth side of our block.

XIV

The Block

The block was born! However, it was just like Swiss cheese; via the holes in it you could get access to the large and empty interior. Well, empty it was not, really. In my time there was only one opening in our side of the square and that led to a carpentry. On the North side a building contractor had his yard with his deadly lime pits. If you ever fell into one of these your body would be digested by the quick lime, dying a horrible death. Or so we were told. On the side of the nuns were barracks of the feared *Maréchaussée*, a kind of militarized police, with stables and a dressage field. Really, they should not have needed to do that. Those Brabanters would never revolt; so save your naked swords to beat down hungry Amsterdam workers. We Brabanters simply perish when needed or unavoidable. A candy store on the one corner, on another corner a coffee, tea and tobacco store, run by Black Betty, where all *Maréchaussée* men could buy on credit. Betty always got her money; she never worried about that, because she had her 'arrangements' with the officers. On the other corner a real steam cleaning shop with a true chimney. Then that fourth side, the one with the inn opposite the presbytery with its high windows that always seemed to frown upon the world. Behind the inn the shooting range, where men practiced their bows and arrows.

A world all unto itself, that block. Populated by all kinds of people, including shy young men and innocent young virgin girls, who knew nothing but who were nevertheless hoping for something like a sweet future. My *Opa* knew it so well and he warned me repeatedly as he had undoubtedly also warned his sons: "They are all sweet young maidens, but where are then all these rotten women coming from?" He had learned already long before that no matter how hard we men try, it will always be not good enough.

In that block my father had been sired – in fact also my mother – and not very much later my brothers and I were born in that same block. I should have been the last one. The family physician had been crystal clear to my father (with my mother as witness) the moment I was born: "This is your last one, because if there is another baby your wife will quite possibly not survive that". Then a book had entered our home. Written by Dr. Huddleton Slater. It was titled "the Tides". We had a bookcase with doors and locks, so it was predicated that I should get into it, which indeed I succeeded in. However, in the meantime another baby had been born. I had hastily been shoved off to my grandparents for an improvised sleeping-over. The next day I was shown the new baby. I was as disappointed as my mother because it was a boy again and we both had hoped very much for a baby girl. With aunt Sientje I had made a special pilgrimage to the Antwerp Zoo to talk to the stork, asking for a little sister. The stork had crabbed with his right paw into the sand to indicate that he had understood. And now this! Even more worrying was the enormous stack of blood-soaked bedsheets I had seen in the kitchen. What exactly had gone wrong with the planning I never found out; clearly the book and the thermometer had not been able to prevent this. The seed had shown itself stronger; my mother had nearly died.

XV

HBS and Military Service

When I graduated from the HBS with very nice grades, it did not do me any good. I had even obtained a 100% University Scholarship for the Agricultural University at Wageningen. However, my parents had told me to refuse that Scholarship. It was actually my mother who was behind this. Her refrain: "This is nothing for us kind of people. This will make you too uppity", was well known by now. In the neighboring city there was, however, an Institute where they formed teachers for the secondary schools. In the end I was allowed to enroll there. It was close by, some 30 km, so I could easily go there by bicycle while continue living at home. All this according to my mother. The Institute and its training was fine enough but I had not counted on the loneliness it entailed. At school I did not have any real friends, but at least I had class mates to talk to on a daily base. Now I had nothing, no one at all. My former class mates had spread all over to various kinds places of higher education; I never saw any of them anymore. That first Christmas after Graduation I stood crying in the back of the church. I had not wanted to go at all, but perhaps God wanted to meet me there. However, he still did as if I did not exist.

It became clear to me very soon, that I had to leave home, as soon as possible. I even concluded that I had to leave Brabant. I had to find a strange, foreign place in order to find myself. I tried to earn some money by giving lessons to private students. Money always was the gate to freedom. I wanted to go very badly to a real University, so I needed money. I did the exams for the teachers certificates for which I had studied three years and then I immediately enrolled myself at the University of Leyden. Finally away from home. Was this the point where I would really become a man?

Yes, indeed, be it in a totally different way than expected. The Minister of Defense thought that I had to serve my country. My study was completed, or so he thought; I thought I had to start. This was terrible! That brute cadaver discipline of the Army! This really was incomprehensible I thought. What could be gained by first treating the new soldiers like dogs or worse? Would they really become better soldiers that way? I thought that the terminology "cadaver discipline" came from the Germans but I soon found out differently. Already in the time of my *Opoe* I had studied German officers and their soldiers through the window of my *Opoe*' living room. They had requisitioned the girls school next to the convent. Wow, they were cleaning all the time! Not only their boots were shining, the whole play area, the corridors, the staircases; everything shone. If a soldier would trip and fall, an officer was immediately next to him, in order to help him up. Yes, there was a lot of shouting; those Germans seem to be incapable of speaking at a normal sound level, that is true. However, never did I hear dirty language. Yes, they did a lot of very loud singing. Under the guidance of a *Herr Oberkapellmeister* naturally, that was true as well.

After the Liberation the English Army had taken over that school; within a few weeks it became one massive disaster. Fires were lit on the floors of the classrooms, all garbage was thrown on a giant heap on the play area (and never removed). I never saw any cleaning activity. I did see lots of broken windows, door from their hinges or without doorknobs; total neglect in short.

Now I was in military service and I had to endure all kinds of humiliation. "It is not your girl! Go and lay right down on your rifle! You think that rifle is clean? Three times undressing and dressing and every time presenting yourself here. You have got 30 minutes! Go and present yourself to the Major, but be sure to first put a cork into your ass, because the Major likes young soldier boys!"

After the basic infantry training I thought I could make myself extra useful by applying to the Commando School. The heavy physical training suited me; I was strong and did not mind getting stronger yet and very fit. The training also involved sabotage and other typical Commando techniques. However, there came also the point where we were taught killing enemy, and doubts began to evolve. Would I be capable of killing somebody in two seconds flat by creeping up to him silently and then slice his throat? I concluded that when given the order I would do it, if it became necessary, but that I rather would be doing something else. So, I asked for a discharge; I was transferred to the Officers' School of the Ordnance Corps. Unfortunately, the discipline problem at this School was even worse. The entire training staff had been trained themselves in England with the English discipline. Their basic discipline tenet is: "First you kick anyone's ass below your rank, because any man above you will surely do the same to you".

All of a sudden we were all officers and all these harassing adjutants and sergeants suddenly sprang to attention and greeted with the military salute as soon as they saw you. Next we were all given a commission somewhere and the true military life began. I became the supply officer in a Company that repaired heavy materiel such as tanks and guns. A most responsible job. I was to make sure that I had the required spare parts so that my colleagues could carry out the repairs. Easy! There were fist-thick books were all the parts of say our tanks were shown, complete with descriptions. Such as: "Pin split to pin firing to breech block to canon 105 How, version pulled, No. 102-455.3456789, number: 6". That meant that I was supposed to have six of them in my stores, but in fact I had none. Therefore quickly a delivery order was made up for the base depot, together with orders for hundreds of other spare parts for this same piece of artillery I was supposed to have while in fact I had none. Proudly I signed all these order forms. However, then the order came back with a tiny little heap of spare parts. The remainder they did not have, not even in this base depot. When would the other parts arrive? Nobody could tell me. Perhaps never or whenever the next instalment of Marshall Aid would arrive. And that again was a moot point because the US was threatening to stop all Marshall Assistance if the Netherlands would not *pronto* transfer New Guinea to Indonesia. Oh, you perhaps thought that Marshall Aid was supposed to help repair all damages our country had sustained during the war? That indeed also happened, here and there. The main reason was, however, that the American weapons manufacturers had stacks of unsold goods, therefore much of the Aid was paid out in weapons. Next they could manipulate the receivers politically. Of course, from a rational point of view the Dutch Government acted within its rights; in *Realpolitik* principles don't count.

No problem; there were about half a dozen pieces of 105 howitzers waiting for repairs. If we just would cannibalize one or two of these, all the others could be repaired. My colleagues looked at me with a pitying smile. I was in the Army, I was told, and the Army had its own logic. For example, there was an Army Corps standing order forbidding all forms of cannibalizing. Well, let us hope that the Russians would stay away a little bit longer, because we had a stock of unusable military hardware that any banana republic dictator would be drooling about, a stock that we were not allowed to repair. No problem again. I requisitioned a jeep with driver and took off in search of some dumps. The Allies had left behind much of their war materials, usually sold for one cent per kilo as if it were scrap. Now I could take the required parts from that materiel, meaning I had to pay the full commercial prices for whatever I took. All from the taxpayer's money, of course. Take it or leave it.

Hurrah again! Suddenly I had become a real man. I was doing something useful and it worked! I was helped by an understanding Company commander, who had been trained in the USA and who had totally different ideas about, for example, discipline. Results, that was what counted, and how you could motivate each other to get optimum results in the shortest amount of time. And he knew how to help these young and inexperienced officers. Of course, I made mistakes once and a while; it is impossible to know everything about leadership immediately. Most definitely so, when you had arrived from the Great Loneliness, where you had almost no social contacts. Believe it or not, I seriously considered signing up extra time in the Army; eventually the other urge, to enter the Infinite Temple of Wisdom, called Graduate University, did win. I just had to go there. I had lost already many years, so I would have to work very hard in order to catch up with my age group.

XVI

St. Augustine

The Military Service had also been of great help in a totally different way. Being an officer, I had drawn a real salary. True, costs for lodging and food were deducted, but every month a neat little sum of money was left over. I saved like the proverbial squirrel. By the time I left the Military I had quite a nice fat bank account, which gave me independence for the rest of my time as a student.

At Leyden I sought some social company with the Catholic Student Society St. Augustine. The famous all-male Leyden Student Corps sounded not attractive. I was 23, I was a sworn Officer in the Netherlands Army, and now I would have my head shorn by some immature Corps Balls? I thought not. Even the much milder co-ed St. Augustine got too much for me. They had some real Greening Nights, where I would have to appear. A number of nerds, not only member of St. Augustine but also of the infamous Corps came especially for an evening of free tormenting.

"Hey, you there", and right away I felt the round end of a walking stick around my neck, "come here". I freed myself from the cane and walked to its owner, who had stood behind me. I told him that I would gladly talk to him, provided this would happen in a civilized manner. Well, well, this totally was not what this Corps Ball had in mind. He roared, scolded, compared me to various beings from the animal kingdom and then demanded that I would shine his shoes. I quickly got fed up with this bastard, walked up closer to him and wrenched the cane from his hands. I next laid the cane over some stair steps, stepped on it so that it broke in two and then said to him: "Please, here is your cane, my name is Gus van der Molenschot. If you want to talk to me you are welcome for a cup of coffee. I live there and there", and then I walked away.

I walked on into a larger room where more pestering and tormenting took place. A dwarf approached me, again with a raised walking cane. I told him that I had just broken a similar cane in two and that I was not enamored by his foul language. He continued scolding and tormenting. Have you ever noticed how amongst the handicapped persons there is a disproportionate number of real nasty people? This was my first experience with this phenomenon. This little monster seemed to draw his power from the perception that nobody would touch him; after all he was deformed and who would want to fight with him? No, I did not fight him. On the other hand I was getting fed up with his foul language, which had nothing to do with the ideals of St. Augustine or with being Catholic. Therefore I opened one of the very large windows, lifted this kobold up in the air and threw him out through that window. He never returned, not then, not later. He had surely survived this treatment, although the windows of these patrician homes at the Rapenburg are quite a bit above street level.

In spite of this I was nevertheless invited to attend the solemn inauguration of all the new members of St. Augustine. We, the new members-to-be, were called in one by one into the room were the entire Executive was standing, dressed in tails (or cocktail dress for the ladies). I too was wearing tails, for this one time I did not mind playing along. My turn came and the chairman – oops, sorry, I mean of course the *praeses* – spoke to me: "Yes, serious doubts had been raised concerning my suitability as a member. However, in the end the Executive had decided to accept me as a member". I stood there with the biggest possible grin on my face, not saying a word. Next I had to pass along the reception line. All executive members stood at the ready to give me the ultimate accolade consisting of a very queer handshake. It consisted of reaching out with the arm and then bending down the fingers and the hand as far as possible. The receiver was then supposed to grip just those bent-down fingers and give them a little squeeze. At the time this was considered the *summum* of Leyden fancy. I did not think a Netherlands Army Officer ought to lower himself to such decadent behavior. Therefore I bent those fingers first back to a normal position and then gave them a solid handshake. What really set the tongues moving afterward, however, that was something quite different. The Executive had two female members and they too stood at the ready with their folded-down hand. For them I had a special treatment. I knelt down for them (on one knee, of course; only God gets both knees!) I then took their pseudo lame hand and kissed it while murmuring: "Mrs. *vice-praeses*" or whatever her function was. Once more I had met two Marias. It happened quite spontaneously, inspired entirely by the carnivalesque show to which I was prepared to add something. It was sarcasm and earnest in one. I cannot even say that I designed it; it just happened in the spur of the moment. You might say that it came from the bottom of my Brabantine soul.

XVII

Studying and no Sex

My studies proceeded fast and effectively. One after the other came the exams, all successful at the first attempt. And again I met Lotte. She had become *praeses* of the Philosophy of Science Niels Stensen Dispute that was part of the St. Augustine umbrella Society. Never before had a female student held such a high position in a Leyden University Dispute. I was deeply impressed. She was not only beautiful to the eye, she had also brains. During a festivity of the Dispute in a restaurant *cum* play garden I had gotten her on the swing and if you managed that you were practically engaged. We saw each other every week during Sunday Mass at St. Augustine. After Mass we all went to "*De Turk*" a renowned restaurant in the *Breestraat* right next to the Student Corps building. We then ordered a small coffee, which was served with all possible *égards* on a silver plate, complete with napkin and a small glass of water (no, not for drinking, stupid, for your fingers!) The price for all this was 45 cent and with a generous gesture you added a 5 cent tip, which was just as graciously accepted by the waiter. This good man knew full well that someday these rat-poor students would return as bank director or some such high functionary and then it would be pay day. The friendship with Lotte remained very distant, however. First study, then get the degree, then find a job.

Not surprisingly, I became an avid member of this Philosophy of Science Dispute Niels Stensen. I always had an interest in the history of the exact sciences and the philosophy of these sciences fitted seamlessly with that. Whenever you do that, then it is only one small step away from the old Greeks and from philosophy in general. I enlisted in a course on Philosophy of Science and later I decided to add this discipline to my academic program in Chemistry and Physics. Let me make it clear that in doing all this I would also see more of this Lotte girl.

Slowly the phenomenon "woman" began to get a practical aspect in my thoughts. Naturally, at some time I hoped to get engaged, get married even, have children and, and, and ….. Would perhaps this Lotte be the one? Let me tell a few things about going steady among Catholic young people. This was around 1955 and the Pill was still far away. Those responsible for our upbringing had done a good job in preparing us for the meeting of the sexes. We were, so we were told, the knights on the white horse, charged with protecting all girls and women. And to never ever bring them into problems. And certainly no sex before marriage. That was almost unheard of in our circles. To make a girl pregnant was about the worst you could do as young man. It would bring eternal shame to two families, a shame which could stretch over several generations. We, young men, were therefore trained in abstaining and resisting all temptations. Those desires could be very strong indeed as I had already experienced myself endlessly. There was also a support system of kinds, consisting of parents and family traditions and of honor. In addition there were also spiritual leaders around us such the priests. Don't underestimate either our personal religiosity as a source of strength by way of our convictions and prayers. It was never explained to us how to deal with our sexuality except that we were taught that masturbation was a mortal sin. The only practical advice we ever received was that we should pray a lot.

The second pillar of our personal defense system was the adoration of the idea "woman" in the best Maria-ish traditions of the Church. Not only were all woman already semi-holy to begin with, they were always beautiful, pure, kindhearted and lovely, always the subject and object of our love, always looking for our manly support. All women were also already the mothers of our yet to be begotten children. Being honorable and courtly towards women was second nature to us. We placed them on pedestals just as we did with Maria, Jesus' mother. All women were Marias, so simple was it. Women were clearly superior to us men. We did not quite understand the so-called women's emancipation. If they wanted, they surely could have all positions in society hitherto held by men. However, they should not become men in the process. After all, the example we men had set was nothing to be proud of. Al we had done over the centuries was killing each other by the millions. As far as I was concerned they were welcome to run the world. Who knows they might well do a lot better than we had done for so many centuries.

XVIII

Lotte

This is how Lotte came into my life, slowly but with strangling certainty. From her side no show of sympathy, certainly no friendship. In this early beginning I was just someone she knew and to whom she talked sometimes. However, even that was already exceptional because Lotte had never had any boyfriend. She had a number of female friends including the strikingly beautiful *blondine* Elly, who was also a Math student in the same year. They worked together on the same exams, working out lecture notes. Elly was forever being asked for dates by her many admirers, attempts she did definitely not encourage. Actually, Lotte was also popular but in a different way. Everybody liked her but that is where it remained. Why was she never asked for a date? Lotte did have some female friends through her VVSL year dispute. This VVSL or Society of Women Students at Leyden was the female counterpart of the Leyden Student Corps, the male bastion. Virtually all female Leyden student were VVSL member, often combined with a membership in one of the confessional student societies. All new VVSL members were forcibly member in one or more of the VVSL Disputes and Year Clubs. These first-year VVSL members usually found their own Disputes. Often clubs where their mothers had already been member of. Sometimes new Disputes were formed; *clique* formation was rife of course. On the other hand these Disputes often were the origin of life-long friendships.

It happened every year again that several girls were not invited by any existing Dispute and then the Executive interfered. In such cases these outcasts were forcibly thrown together and ordered to form a new Dispute. In this way every new VVSL member became a member of at least one Dispute. To no-one's surprise Lotte ended up in this *Salon des Refusées*. She simply did not have the social acumen or the 'connections' to work her way up. Therefore Lotte ended up in one of these enforced new Disputes and later I got to know the other members of this Dispute. It was a very strange collection. One was an albino; not a bad person at all, but nevertheless strange in several respects. However, she was respected if only because she developed herself as an able academic in spite of her physical handicap. The remainder could best be described as dikes, *excusez le mot*. Even if they weren't they would probably soon become one, because much femininity they did not possess. In that time being different was not accepted. I hope for them that later they would form entirely stable lesbian relationships. Lotte did not belong in that group; for the second time she was an outcast. You could say about Lotte what you wanted but not that she would have any lesbian inclination. Man hater, yes, absolutely; women she did not like any better. Probably she liked nobody, least of all herself. There was indeed something wrong with Lotte's femininity, but that lay on a totally different level.

XIX

Engaged?

"Lotte, here is a ring. Would you accept it and marry me?"

How did I get to this point? It is near impossible to reconstruct. A resultant of many small happenings, which stringed together like a rosary. Who seduced whom? I knew full well what enticed me so much, quite apart from the erotic feelings she awakened in me. On the other hand Lotte's desires and designs remained an enigma to me. A little while later she said: "I want an oak tree to lean against". This should have warned me but the opposite happened. Here was a "damsel in distress" and it was clear that she needed protection and salvation; she needed a knight on a white horse and I wanted to be that knight wholeheartedly. The warning was that she never said that she liked me or something like it; she only talked about her own want list. Much later I came to the conclusion that even at that early time she must have been already psychologically entirely loony, too hung up to ever been able to sustain a normal man-woman relation. Who knows, those other young men perhaps had instinctively sensed a sick spirit, of which even the carrier herself may have had little inkling. I ought to have sensed that too; however, if I had an subconscious understanding, then I was still blinded by her nectar. And the perceived call of the sirens who appealed to this noble page. Whatever my reserves may have been, I fell head over heels for this nymph. Ho, wait a minute! Was that a Freudian slip of the tongue? Was I talking about a nympho?

I really thought that I was very much in control of my life. True, I was systematically carrying out my plans and I was indeed successful in that. Lotte was going to take a certain position in those plans. However, for that part to succeed I first had to win her over for me and then I had to ask her in marriage. Probably, quite likely even, I had been seduced already myself, not realizing that I had been caught in Lotte's fishing net. "Let it be just Gus". Had she really been thinking that? In the meantime it was still a long time removed from a marriage proposal.

For sure Lotte herself was a vat full of problems. At least at the moment we got to know each other. It didn't take long or I began to hear about these. Her big problem was her mother. Her mother who had managed to take away and to destroy the love her oldest daughter had felt for her. "Now I cannot love my mother any more", she cried at my chest, leaning against her oak tree. I could not solve that problem for her but I could give her my love and in this way let her know that she counted for something. I hoped to give her a bit more self-confidence because clearly that was lacking with her. That was not only due to her mother although she let no opportunity pass to denigrate Lotte: "You are worthless.

You don't even know how to peel a potato. You better become a school teacher or something like that because surely you will never catch a man. Look at that frumpy dress you are wearing. You really have no sense of taste." There was another point. Lotte was teaching Mathematics part time at an MMS, a rather low level secondary school system for girls. How do you motivate silly young cows, who didn't have the brains for anything academic and who were in school only because the Education Law required this? Mathematics, of all things! Naturally Lotte had problems to keep order amongst this unruly bunch. Next she would fall ill again every time she had to teach. When she was a teenager herself, still falling under compulsory education, she had reacted by obtaining only A and A+ marks. This way she remained in the goods books with her mother. Now, all of a sudden this was all no longer good enough. Then, on top of it all she was the oldest child at home where she was charged with a sense of responsibility towards all these brothers and sisters.

Gerard was the second child in the Ten Brink family. He had fled from the Senior Seminary. Well, actually, he had been sent away because he could not tame his sexual urges, in spite of praying, self-chastising and other forms of torture. In the eyes of his father, who understood nothing of such urges, he had committed treason by giving up his studies towards the priesthood. His mother understood him much better. She adored this son, whom she thought to be a genius and to whom she often turned for advice. Did she perhaps in this son recognize some of her own sexual needs? Was he perhaps the kind of man she had never had but had always longed for? An Oedipus situation then? Did Gerard feel likewise? The strange thing was (strange because Gerard was the only child exempted from the compulsory love for the mother) that Gerard later on would also show that he was incapable of loving. His sick relation with his wife Aletta we will encounter later on.

Betty was the third one; perhaps she got it even worse than the others, at least during a certain period when Betty was still at home. According to Ma Betty was good for nothing because she was too stupid. That is why Betty had been sent to a *Mulo* school, a school type of even lower academic stature than an MMS, designed for the slightly mentally retarded, who were too young to be married away to throw babies, but who had to be parked somewhere. How totally wrong Ma had been in her assessment would become clear later on when Betty, all on her own did the difficult State exams for the HBS school type and in this way forced her way into University where she eventually completed her studies in the Faculty of Medicine. However, first that *Mulo* and staying home, where she got a daily dose of vitriol from her psychotic mother. At a certain point Betty married Henk. It was no secret that this was a so-called St. Joseph marriage. So-called, because Henk was totally impotent and therefore there could be no normal sexual intercourse. The entire family knew about this which is certainly a somewhat strange situation. Stranger yet: why did the Church condone this? The Church has always held that the purpose of marriage is obtaining children. Was this not contrary with the holiness of a

Christian marriage? Well, then it was compared with the vows of the Nuns, who all wore a wedding ring as symbol of their relation with Jesus. It would be stretching things to see it as a punishment by God but it is a fact that Henk died less than a year later in a terrible car accident, whereby this unholy union was abruptly ended. In the meantime Betty had been smart enough not to return to her parental home. First she hired her herself out to a business woman who needed assistance with her children. This soon ended when the relation with her employer became somewhat too close for comfort. Betty moved to Groningen where she started her medical studies. She lived with a house mate, but when this other women wanted a Lesbian relationship an enormous row ensued, because Betty did not want that. Later I wondered if Betty would not have been happier in a lesbian relation. In any case there was something not quite in order with Betty's relations with men. Yet later again she ended up in a marriage of convenience by marrying a widower with four wild teenage daughters. Always suffering, always doing penance for the sins she did never commit. How well do I know that theme! Betty was looking for Love but never got beyond the point of some degree of affection.

The three latecomers in the Ten Brink family were too young to be witness to Ma's difficult menopause so they had it a lot easier. In the middle there was another daughter who had been sent to a boarding school in her teenage years, somewhere far away. There she had also contracted psychological damages but in any case she had been spared the influence of Ma ten Brink.

This third daughter called Geesje was a real 'teach', with the label of 'pseudo-intellectual' quite visibly pasted on her forehead. Never a deep thought would escape from there, but that is perhaps the reason that she was reasonably happy in her life. She married a much older man (Oedipus again?) from a low blue collar environment and she did her utmost to never want to outgrow her social strata. In this she was the only one of the seven. Perhaps her solution to a never enunciated problem.

XX

Break-up

In this considerably dysfunctional family I ended up. It took a while before I was allowed to have my maiden visit to the Rotterdam family. Actually, Lotte seemed to be happy with her boyfriend. Perhaps not necessarily with this particular one but rather with the fact that she had one. She never showed her happiness in any romantic fashion. No, we were just going steady and what did that entail? Not much more than a non-verbal agreement that we were exclusively going out with each other. Perhaps we would walk hand in hand or arm in arm. Perhaps a little kiss on the cheek; that was all. Remember, we young men had to protect the honor of our girls. My happiness, however, was complete. This was the woman for the rest of my life. There were still some two years of hard university work ahead of me, but after that a solid income was beckoning and with that a chance to get married. What and how was Lotte really feeling about it all? I must admit that I really did not know for sure, but somehow she seemed to like it. I was a bit disconcerting that these little kisses always were at my initiative, never hers. She did not say much about it and she never really answered any questions about it. Should I have been given deeper meaning to anything at that time already? Her conduct was rather clear. She was really clinging and wanted to be always near me. "We can study together, can't we?" She could never quite understand that a man with a steady erection cannot at the same time concentrate on the structure of the universe or whatever exam I was presently working on. And from my part I could not, no, I was not allowed to tell her of my sexual arousal. "Only on Sunday", I stipulated, "and perhaps on Wednesday for lunch". To avoid misunderstanding; I was not talking about having sex.

In those days such an understanding was not uncommon; there were plenty of couples in love or even engaged who saw each other perhaps only once a week or less. The wisdom of those days was that this would actually strengthen the bond. For Lotte this was impossible. Every time I heard her click-clack of her heels on the pavement. "Only ten minutes" she then promised; however, those ten minutes often became two hours and then my whole evening was spoiled and waisted. Waisted indeed because I was in a hurry having lost already some five years before I finally got to the University, and that loss of time I now wanted to recuperate. We poor boys did not have the luxury of social activities, not even of friendships. At all times we had to work like slaves towards that future, in order to exorcize the spectre of poverty. A poverty that for the present I accepted voluntarily. My luxury consisted of one pouch of pipe tobacco a week and that famous one cup of coffee in *De Turk*.

And so, with all that feeling of love in my heart, the doubts and the despair came over me. On a fateful day I told Lotte with bleeding heart that I wanted to break up our relation. I was very sad but also relieved and with renewed energy I immersed myself in my studies and other tasks. Lotte was not as much saddened as angry. That should have told me something. For her it was back to the *Salon des Refusées*.

XXI

Verona and Thereafter.

However, at that moment I was not seeing it that way. Nor could I even dream that some forty years later a very similar situation would develop. In the mist of my sorrow I perhaps perceived a little bit of it; in my mind it was something that had to happen. The relation was interfering with my studies and without those studies I would never be able to have a real relation. My mentors had been right once more; studies and women did not mix. That too was an absolute truth in those days. At that time I had not yet been in Rotterdam to meet my future in-laws. Over there everyone was also angry. Because of the insult against their daughter. Listen Ma, haven't you been justified? According to you she was good for nothing, right? You have just been proven right, Ma!

The adventures at Venice and Verona were not forgotten. How did I then arrive in this shit heap? I had been so terribly happy. When I had gotten home I had written her a letter; she still had holiday and therefore she stayed with her parents. I tried to be funny by drawing little doodles, little figures that attempted to convey a message, be it rather cloaked messages. Hurrah, it worked! After about two weeks she arrived. She actually came to my digs and rang the doorbell. I quickly showed her my best easy chair (fifteen guilders from the recycle shop) and she even allowed me to kiss her. I kissed her on the forehead and then a cheek, because that is wat I had seen Gary Grant and Deborah Kerr do in the movies. It took a few weeks before she allowed us to be seen as a pair in public. At long last we were walking arm in arm in the streets for the whole world to see. She struggled mightily against this, leaving me to conclude that I had to conquer her. Of course we were seen, which had been my intention, and probably hers too, but at the time I was too naïve to notice.

While I was in seventh heaven somewhere else, somebody else went through hell. On a certain day, or evening rather, Leo came to visit me unannounced. Remember? Leo had been the *vice-praeses* of the Niels Stensen Dispute where Lotte was the *praeses* and he had persuaded me to become the next *vice-praeses*.

"Can I talk to you for five minutes?"
"Please come in".
"Is it true that Lotte and you are going together?"
"Yes, that is true but why would you want to know?"
Then his whole story came out. That he was in love with Lotte for years already, but that she had never shown any sign of interest. On the other hand he had never told her of his feelings for her, afraid to be rejected. He kept hoping that something mutual

would develop spontaneously; nothing of the kind had ever happened. It had never occurred to him how mindless his approach had been. If he never took any initiative, how then could he expect Lotte to show any affection?

I told Leo the story of "The Lord of Jericho", a novel by Edmund Nicolas; at the time a widely read and admired book. The story is about a man of old nobility, living in Limburg. He has spent most of his life pursuing a certain woman. He could not get it through his head, that actually she wanted him too, but she wanted to be conquered, kidnaped, maybe or preferably even pulled around by her hair and violated. Anything except his repeated and very polite proposals. Much later, our friend then is already way beyond his prime, he gets the idea. He is spending an evening with his friend, the village priest, enjoying a good cigar and an excellent wine. Our shepherd knows he has to say something sensible to help his friend, but he does not even know the subject. Therefore he throws out all kinds of loose talk, hoping that something will hit home. Suddenly our nobleman jumps up and tells the astonished priest that he has to go and must travel immediately to America. There he finds his woman, drags her off (much to her delight) but then when the wedding is being organized, she disappears again, to be kidnaped again by her knight and next she joyfully says "yes" on the altar.

Leo had never understood this. I consider myself a gentleman, but even so I had taken a brave initiative. I had taken her hand, risking that Lotte would send me away. This is how in the end I had won her over. Leo could never bring himself to this point where he might be rejected. Leo therefore also never got to know what disaster he had escaped from. Leo was much too sweet and too nice, even more so than I. The dominant Lotte would have put him through the meat grinder. After our talk Leo wrote me a pathetic letter, once more pouring his sorrow over me. There was nothing I could do for him. At the time I had little wood stove in my room of the type: "*Je brûle tout l'hiver sans m'éteindre*". It was Fall and this little stove gave already some comforting warmth. I opened he top lid and let Leo's letter fall into the flames. His sadness, his hopes went up in flames; only a few small ash shards were left.

Leo was a brilliant scientist and also a very talented violin player. Once he had invited me to his laboratory for lunch and for a solo violin performance. His lab suddenly was filled with a Bach partita, so crystal pure that I really shivered. Through no effort of myself I happen to have an absolute ear; if he would have started a quarter note too low or too high I would have heard it. However, no such thing. Perhaps a bit sharp of tone, the way Jehudi Menuhin used to play, but in a never wavering purity of sound. I never heard Leo again on his violin; I think he was too scared for criticism. A very dominant father had made a doubter of Leo with a considerable inferiority complex. Leo wandered around for many years. Alone and lonely. On a certain moment, however, he had gotten married to a very well-built tall blonde. I have no idea how he managed to do that. I am very glad for him that this is the way it went for him. I know for a fact that his father is dead and that already for many years.

Now I had broken my relation with Lotte. However, we kept seeing each other, if only from the corners of our eyes during Mass at St. Augustine or at "*De Turk*". I was living in a sort of trance. The exams rolled by as a kind of assembly line. In a way it was a happy time; I worked entirely for myself and for my dream. The dream to escape poverty. That is why I wanted that University degree. To escape from that deadly grip of poverty, which had so strongly determined my young years. This may sound ungrateful, because we had at home everything essential. A warm house, fairly neat clothes, enough to eat, good schools and radio for entertainment. However, never anything extra. Across from us in the street a family lived where both parents were unemployed actors. They had barely a chair to sit on, but they had lots of fun. Whenever they had a few extra dimes, that little money was immediately converted into something joyful. Not with us.

All extra dimes went into a savings account, because my father had no pension rights and severe poverty would come his way, when he could not work anymore.

How we enjoyed that chocolate bar which *Oma* sometimes brought along when she had been shopping on the market place. Please understand; one bar only for four boys. How jealous I had been with my school mates who had stockings which had been bought in a store, rather than ours which had been knitted with wool from my *Opoe*'s undershirt. I hated these shirts which too evidently had been made from old bed sheets. I had been so sad when my parents refused me to letting me become a boy scout. That was much too expensive, they said. Think of the uniform, for example. How could I ever escape this strangling lower-white-collar poverty? However, I did find a little escape hatch, a very first little start towards a better life. As always, money was the deciding factor. At the time I was in the fourth year of my HBS secondary school and my savings were exactly ten guilders. How did I ever get so much money? Impossible to save that from the 15 cent weekly spending money I got from my mother. That was so terribly little that I could never ask a girl to the cinema. Or I would save it up for weeks on end. Working for it was also out. There had been several opportunities for work and make some money, especially during the holidays. No, my parents did not allow that either. Such menial work was below their social standing they said; we were too good for that, so was the reasoning.

No, those ten guilders I had found. Right in the street, there it was, a nice ten guilder bank note. Returning it to the owner who had lost it appeared to be impossible. How could any person prove that this bank note had been his or hers, that he first had it and then no longer? I decided that it was a Devine intervention, which by high exception had been in my favor. I therefore kept it, but not for long. At school a notice had been pinned up, saying that a tennis club would be started.

Therefore, with those ten guilders I bought a tennis racket and then presented myself as a member of that club. A mixed club no less! The school Moderator (a priest!) came to watch us a couple of times, because this had never been done before at a Catholic school. At home I had not told my parents anything about those ten guilders; I just presented them with the done fact of the tennis racket purchase. My mother's reaction was very interesting. As if she vaguely understood a bit of my dreams. I think that in a sly way she was pleased that this son tried to work himself into the higher strata of society. Remember that at the time, playing tennis was an elite sport; my club mates were all from the so-called higher classes, children of doctors, lawyers, that kind. "Yes, those gymnastics shoes are worn out. Buy some white ones, that looks better at tennis." Next I got splendid white shorts, as always made from a bed sheet but of a smart modern design, that my mother had copied from her *Beatrijs* magazine. Finally, for my birthday, I was presented with a really beautiful white knitted sweater with a cable motive. I never found out where my mother had gotten the wool from; this time it definitely was new and not from an old undervest. It was really a most beautiful sweater, admired by everyone at the club; it felt a bit as if I suddenly had become a real man.

XXII

Professor B.

"Ah, Monsieur B. Puis-je vous présenter un fameux compatriot de vous? Voici le professeur Auguste van der Molenschot. M. van der Molenschot est actuellement professeur à la Faculté des Sciences à Paris".

The revenge could not have been sweeter. Professor B. had been my doctoral supervisor in my Leyden days. Because of him I had suffered a very humiliating experience. Something that I had never forgiven him. Professor B. is the only human that I have truly ever hated. Even my ex-wife I have never really hated, although she hated me on a large scale, something she told me hundreds of times (more accurately "shouted"). The Leyden years were now far behind me and I was full professor in Canada. If I had been presented as a *professeur de l'université canadien* that would not have had half the effect. 'Professor' in Canada could have meant many things like 'Assistant Professor' or 'Associate Professor'. And frankly speaking what is Canada but a backward ex-colony, compared to the famous Sorbonne *Faculté des Sciences?* The beauty of it all was that it was factually true. I had a temporary appointment at the Sorbonne, the one and only time in my life that I had the pleasure of receiving a double salary.

I had noticed him right away, my professor B., during a reception at the start of a scientific symposium in Nancy, France. I asked a French colleague to introduce me to professor B. not telling him that professor B. and I knew each other already very well. That wasn't necessary, because like all Frenchmen he smelled a conspiracy in the air, and Frenchmen positively adore conspiracies. Without further encouragement or additional information he performed like a pro. Just like the priest in Edmund Nicolas' novel he had no clue about the real story, but guided by pure instinct he did what was expected of him and he did it perfectly.

The memory of professor B. had been fading for a long time, but it had never gone away. Only shortly before the Nancy meeting I had become slightly tipsy during a party at the home of professor K. during a visit to the Netherlands. I had been staying too long, happy with the company of some old friends of long ago. And suddenly it came out like an orgasm: "I hate him, I hate him, I hate him"! While my host tried to calm me down, the others were well aware about whom I was raving. The story was well known. It was some ten years after the humiliating experience; clearly the feeling still had not disappeared. The fire had been burning underground without me actually being aware of it.

Now I had my moment of sweet revenge. Professor B. and I had an aimable bit of small talk as 'amongst colleagues'. He had been member of the Club of Rome and so we talked about its first report and world politics. Naturally Prince Bernhard and his Bilderberg Conferences formed the next logical topic. We talked about Pierre Trudeau of Canada and his remarkable policies *vis*-à-*vis* China and Cuba, not to forget his more ludic actions such as sliding down stair bannisters and turning pirouettes behind the back of Queen of England, all while the TV cameras were turning.

XXIII

Again Together

How come she kept seducing me? Her golden blond curls? Her breasts that she kept showing off with up-lifting bras and tight sweaters as the fashion dictated at that time? Or was it that strong battle within myself, that strong sexual urge I experienced every day? Lotte very carefully avoided looking directly at me, particularly when she knew that I was looking at her. She made sure she would be seen; she always looked very smartly dressed, hair well kept, with blood-red lipstick. Desmond Morris at that time had not yet published his book "the Naked Ape", but the main message from that book I had absorbed long ago. Perhaps not as explicitly and rationally but certainly with my loins.

It became Spring again and everywhere in the parks the crocuses and the daffodils were in bloom. The end of my tunnel came in sight. Only one more important exam plus perhaps another six months of laboratory work and then I would be ready for my doctoral exam. While the saps of life flowed richly and the hormones stormed through my body, I fell again for Lotte's charms. I decided that she had to be my wife after all and that I was going to ask her to marry me.

At a jeweler I bought a golden ring of her size. In a flower shop I bought a bunch of budding chestnut branches, their buds full of vitality and promise and then I asked Lotte for lunch. She accepted! She showed her happiness with the chestnut branches, but when I gave her my little box, asking her to marry me, she hesitated. She looked at the ring, closed the little box and put it into her handbag. She said that she was very honored with my proposal and that she was very pleased with it, but that she had to think about it. She did not reject me but I had expected a bit more enthusiasm. What was there to think about, after all this time? There was no other suitor; of that I had made sure. Nobody else had asked her, even not Leo. Would she rather want to stay forever in that *Salon des Refusées?*

It did not matter much because from that moment onwards we were virtually inseparable. I had now more time for her and we had a good life together. Lotte too had only one more exam to do and together with her best friend Elly she prepared for it. In the meantime I had obtained an appointment as research assistant, where I had to help a senior student who was working on his doctorate thesis. I made a bit of money this way and at the same time I was fulfilling one of the laboratory requirements. Such a doctorate required an extra 4-7 years after the doctoral exam. Perhaps, perhaps, very perhaps I would like to follow that route too. I worked on something extremely esoteric; the refractive index of electrolyte solutions. What could you do with that kind of knowledge? Well, perhaps just understanding Nature and that was enough of a reason to study it. On a morning Lotte came to me in my laboratory. She threw herself into my arms. She had just done that very last and very difficult exam and although the professor had said that it was OK, he had nevertheless demanded that she come back the next day. That would be another awful interrogation lasting many hours. In the end she had been given a mark of "6" on the scale of 1-10, let us say a C grade, barely passing. This had been an incredible blow for Lotte who was used to A and A+ grades. Now, after nine months of hard work, just a naked "6", the lowest mark she had ever gotten (apart from "physical exercise"). I could tell her that this professor had a reputation for being very hard on students. She knew that, of course, and that had been the underlying reason for the collaboration with Elly. I think that at that moment something snapped within her, and that on top of the psychological burden she was already carrying. Ma ten Brink was never very far away, in spite of the physical distance of many kilometers. The pressure that Ma asserted was there always and everywhere. However, the good point was that Lotte was now free to seek a full-time job. She found one down South, not far from my town of birth.

XXIV

Doctoral, but not Really

Not long thereafter I had finished all exams and laboratory requirements. Only the doctoral exam remained. This consisted of five professors asking me all kinds of questions; it was usually a formality but it had to be done. In the meantime I had already found a job, also in the South, where a new University was going to be founded. Just that last *pro forma* exam; unfortunately it turned out to be anything but a *sinecure*. One of my professors had done something he was not allowed to do. He had taken me on as a paid research assistant and that work would count for the six months of laboratory work I was supposed to do. The other professors disagreed. I did pass the exam and then heard that I would not get the diploma and that I first had to do some extra laboratory work. In fact I solved that problem very quickly. I was charged with a project, which I finished in six weeks and then they let me go; I received he diploma in the mail.

The incident left a deep scar. My own main supervisor/professor had sold me down the drain; that was how it felt. He had put his own interests above that of this student. It also turned out that I was not the only one so treated. His colleagues had decided to put an end to these practices. Also not quite kosher, because this war between professors was fought out over my back. When it had finally dawned on me what the matter had really been, I felt a deeply penetrating anger coming up in me. The incident was extra painful because such a doctoral exam is a semi-public event. Usually it is one big party. Parents, family and friends are present in the Aula of the University waiting in pleasant anticipation until the new-fangled *Doctorandus* exits from the famous sweat room. My parents were there, as well as Lotte's parents plus several of her siblings plus a whole bunch of our Leyden study friends. I was staying in that exam room very long, far too long according to normal standards. My supporters became restless and then a kind of worried silence had fallen over the group. Clearly something was wrong but they had no idea what was the matter. At long last the door opened and I came out, stumbling and with a face like death painted over, according to witnesses. Initially I was incapable of speaking; I leaned against the wall, trying to find myself. My friends stood around me: "What has happened? Did you fail? Did you pass? Do you have your doctoral?" It took an awfully long time before I could answer any of these questions. It must have been just as torturing for my environment as for me; finally I found my voice and I began to talk. I explained that the exam itself had gone very well. I had been able to answer all questions satisfactorily and on two points had gotten into a true discussion in which I survived. In fact, at the end the Chairman had given me the highest *iudicium,* which consisted of an official invitation to continue my studies and work toward a full doctorate. On the other hand I had to admit that I had not received my doctoral diploma. I told them the terrible story of Professor B. who had misled me. Unfortunately, Professor B. was not present at the exam and he could not be reached by telephone either. Therefore the professors at hand had to take a difficult decision. From my circle of friends relieved commentary arose: "Oh, if that is all, you will have that diploma anyway in a few weeks. Just a formality. Come on, let us celebrate and party."

XXV

No Love

Nobody really understood why I looked so defeated; there was yet another, deeper reason. This was also the day of our official engagement! At long last Lotte had given me her "yes" word. Finally she had also told me why she had hesitated so much:

"I WANT TO MARRY YOU, THAT IS TRUE. HOWEVER, I HAVE TO TELL YOU THAT I DO NOT REALLY LOVE YOU, AT LAST NOT IN THE WAY LOVE IS SUPPOSED TO EXIST BETWEEN A WOMAN AND THE MAN SHE IS GOING TO MARRY".

I had waved off her doubts. With the reckless self-confidence of the young people I told her that such feelings are quite common amongst brides to be. It was a natural reticence which would surely disappear as soon as she was married to me. She wanted sex, she had said and she wanted babies and I assured her that she would get both. "Wait until you have your first baby. Then you will feel quite different". Lotte let herself be convinced. She had told me and perhaps she had now silenced her conscience. In any case I was happy now and

I will be eternally grateful to her for her frankness. I did not realize that now a great burden had been loaded on my shoulders; from now on it was up to me to make her happy and to ensure she would begin to love me. I did not know that this was a 'Mission Impossible'. After four years of going steady with me she ought to know me reasonably well. If in those years no loving feelings towards me had developed how then these were to arise later? I had my whole being devoted to her and she knew that. What more could I possibly do? We were smart enough to think that our sexuality could contribute to that end, but we also knew that it would be no end in itself and no make-happy elixir. With open eyes but seeing nothing, I entered a future which could only be disastrous. I had no inkling of it at that moment.

In order to save money we had combined my doctoral and our official engagement into one event. Fact is that during that that infamous exam I had been wearing the gold engagement ring that Lotte had given me eventually. Next the whole crowd had moved to my address where the landlady had very kindly put the entire ground floor at our disposal. I remember very little of it. Friends came by to congratulate us, bringing small presents. I still have one or two of these '*Gilde*' wine glasses which we received one by one from our friends. They were all poor, just like me and such a '*Gilde*' glass was both affordable and appropriate. I just sat there with the same thoughts running around in my mind. What was Lotte thinking of all this? I don't know. I don't remember how she reacted to my letdown before that examining committee. She was well aware of the world of the

University; rationally she will have realized that it was really a fight amongst professors and that I would get that piece of paper very soon anyway. However, there stood the man she was going to marry, her oak tree to lean against. On this very important moment he had failed in the presence of many, including her parents. To her credit it must be said that she never came back to it. However, what did she really think in her heart?

XXVI

Prozac

"My husband is insane. Please lock him up. He belongs in a mental institution". This is Lotte, screaming in front of my psychiatrist. It is now some thirty years later and saying that much had happened in the intervening years is perhaps the understatement of the century. I had been ill, indeed, but that was past tense. A deep depression had taken hold of me. However, somehow I had gotten out of it, be it that it did cost me many years of my life. Prozac had been the Great Savior. Bit by small bit I had made progress, mostly through my own efforts, and now Prozac had given me the last, very sweeping push. At the time Prozac was new in Canada and I had asked my psychiatrist if I might try it. In the United States the introduction of Prozac had been tumultuous, to say the least. Sensation-seeking TV programs had taken hold of it and an entire continent watched in fascination. There were accusations that it would encourage suicide. Not true. Prozac, like all anti-depressives, requires time to get effective, usually 3-6 weeks after the start. "Yes, my brother was prescribed Prozac and ten days later he was dead! You are murderers!"

"No, Missus, you were just too late. If you had put him on Prozac a few weeks earlier he would probably been alive to-day." Great TV, poor science. On me the effect of Prozac had been dramatic. Here I was, physically and mentally a total wreck, a shadow of the man I had ever been, barely able to utter a few words, incapable of walking more than five steps at the time, before being forced back into my wheelchair. I could not read or watch TV. Yes, I could watch but nothing would stay. Personalities or a story line never were clear. Music did not exist anymore for me. Whenever I tried radio or CD player I heard the sound but it was a cacophony, without any connection. Speaking was not much better; only some short, one-dimensional sentences would come out. A plus B leading to C was already beyond me. Finances I had long ago turned over to my wife; I could not even write a proper cheque anymore. I spoke in a very slow cadence and I walked deeply bent over, leaning on a cane. And always there was pain, chronic pain in my back. Not just the pain shoots that made you scream, but also the gnawing chronic pain that drove me mad, just like the Chinese water torture.

And now with Prozac all that began to recede like the clouds after a heavy rain storm. Initially very slowly so, but after six weeks my environment even began to notice it. "You are walking much straighter", I heard them say. If, for the first time you walk ten meters rather than five, nobody notices. When you can walk through the entire shopping center without having to sit down every two minutes for a rest, then everyone realizes that something special is happening. For myself the most dramatic difference was that I could speak again and could take part in conversations again. After three months I took over the finances; the cheques I could produce again without mistake. Only one thing spoiled my joy about these rapid improvements. Lotte was not happy at all, quite to the contrary. She stated that I had become manic. She had never read anything about psychiatry so where these sudden insights came from was not clear. However, I saw an opportunity here and I invited her to join me next time I saw my psychiatrist. After all these years she yielded and for the first (and also last) time she entered a psychiatrist' place.

"My husband has gone crazy. He is completely insane. He does not know anymore what he is doing. You have to do something about it". He replied: "Your husband is completely normal and healthy; there is nothing wrong with him. He is completely sane and he knows perfectly well what he is doing". "Then both of you are crazy", Lotte screamed. "You both belong in the madhouse". She ran up to the psychiatrist and began to pummel his chest with her fists, while stomping her feet. I quietly watched the whole scene. No need for me to say anything. My good doctor would have loved to keep Lotte in for a talk and a test, but no chance; Lotte ran out to the car. I too would have loved if Lotte had taken that personality test; another missed opportunity.

Back at home Lotte did not allow me this small victory. She went straight into the offensive, claiming that Prozac was destroying me. "Yes, Lotte, the treatment with Prozac has changed your husband profoundly. He was a total wreck, almost catatonic, and now he has improved in all respects. He can walk again, he can make conversation again, and therefore he can think again, so where are you so excited about?"

She tried to even get the children involved in her fight. Astrid, our number two said: "Yes, Papa, even your voice is different now". "Yes, my child, you are eighteen now and you have known mostly a sick father during the last 10-12 years. You don't even remember how your father used to sound. This is your real Papa".

In this way I had to introduce myself again to my environment and even to my own children. Later, much later I heard that my oldest daughter had set up her mother against me with wildly exaggerated, mostly untrue stories about Prozac. The attacks simply never stopped. Finally I said: "Listen, Lotte, I am going to Europe, to the Netherlands, all by myself. I will prove to all of you that I can do that without any problems, mistakes or accidents". "Ha, you cannot even do that. You will lose your way and probably will get killed".

Lotte did not agree, but I bought a ticket and departed. Why was Lotte so angry? Why was she not pleased by my recovery? Her story that I had become manic was pure nonsense. She did not even know what being manic meant in practice; she absolutely had no knowledge about such matters. All she would have to do was to simply look at me, listen to me and watch me and especially listen to the people around me to know that I was simply just recovering from whatever the illness was that I had suffered from for all those years. I was alert again, full of joy and vitality with a suddenly revived interest in everything beautiful in life. However, my wife could not accept this. Why not, Lotte? Did you prefer to see me sick, weak and handicapped? Why was my recovery causing fear in you?

During the next four weeks I did what any normal tourist would do. I borrowed a car and every day was an adventure. Before I got into my car, I studied the maps, put the information into my brains and then went on my way. Not once during these weeks did I lose my way or did my memory fail me in any way. The Netherlands were really new to me. During the last 25 years a whole new net of highways had been built and I had to learn quickly. Family and friends were glad and excited. To be true I still walked with a cane and I used Prozac and Lithium but my mind was clear. Once again I could remember everything and above all I was capable of enjoyment again. The deadly chronic pain also went to the background and I did not have a single attack of intense pain shoots.

Filled with joy I flew back to Canada. Only to be met by an icy reception from Lotte, who initially listened to my happy tales in dead silence. Lotte was not happy at all with my positive experiences. In fact she was hopping mad. It took only a little while or she exploded. I cannot really repeat all she said but it was the same story again. How I humiliated her and so forth. Then, screaming she ran up the stairs, only to come down again two days later. Suddenly she claimed I had had a sexual affair with my sister-in-law Aletta during my stay in the Netherlands. Aletta had been the wife of Lotte's oldest brother, but was separated. Indeed I had stayed a few days at the home of Aletta and her brother, as I had stayed also with other friends. And always without any sexual escapades.

XXVII

Unfaithful?

This was not the end, not even the end of the beginning but the beginning of the end, to paraphrase Winston Churchill. During the next three years Lotte came with a list of 32 women with whom I was supposed to have had a sexual relation. A veritable effort besting Don Juan, if it had been true. Included was the sister-in-law in the Netherlands; the remainder were all Canadian. "These are only the women I am absolutely certain about. I have the proof! I will say nothing about the others whom I also suspect. And then of course there are the many I know nothing about".

The women she mentioned by name were all from our own social circle. Most of them we knew already 10-20 years, all honorable women with nothing against them. What can you do with such accusations? The first one you shove aside: "Don't be ridiculous, Lotte. I have never even touched that woman, let alone having had sex with her". That made no impression at all. Next I challenged her: "You say you have proof. Show me your evidence". "Yes, I saw you talking with Mrs. X. I saw how she looked at you and then I knew".

After thirty years of marriage we had ended up in this impasse. It did not happen all of a sudden. We got married in 1960, a very special time. In the Netherlands and perhaps in the other European countries as well, we were just then crawling out of the second world war and its aftermath. Not only did we get new bridges, new roads and new buildings, also new civil institutions were created, new means of communication and rapidly a totally new look on the future developed. The first signs of a new society were already discernable. I had been appointed at a brand new University, the first of a whole group that would rapidly change the academic world in the Netherlands. The contraceptive Pill had been invented, although initially we Catholics were not allowed to use them. However, many disobeyed that and after our Bishop *Monseigneur* Bekkers declared that this was a matter for the individual conscience, the use of the Pill became universal. Like ourselves, millions of couples decided to go with the Pill, with drastic results. It was no longer required to have these very large families with eight or twelve children. Generally it was found that three or four children was just nice. And so these large families disappeared without so much as a whisper.

As a result the women had more time. Why then not take a job, perhaps part time, so that there was some extra money for holidays, a nicer home or even a small car? That the women in this way also got more power in their marriage, well, that was a nice side effect. Collateral damage, some would say.

XXVIII

Married

Therefore we got married, after first having worked and saved some money. We bought a home, be it with an 80% mortgage. With a fixed 4% interest rate for 30 years we were really sitting on roses, so to speak. I had a permanent job at this new University and Lotte had a part time job teaching in the secondary school system. Soon the first baby announced itself while I was hoping and saving for our first car. It became a real race; Lotte with her baby and I with my car. I don't recall who won, except that it was close towards the end.

For all the signs we were swimming in happiness; all our dreams were coming true at long last. We had worked very hard for it and we had to wait very long for it to happen. Lotte and I both had a bit a conservative outlook on life. First save, then buy. We still both went to church every Sunday, we had remained virgin for all of our premarital life. No sex before marriage; at the time that was a strong tabu. At the same time that was a problem because we both wanted sex, I for one was about to burst at the seams. Fine, my friend, but then you first get married. I did not know, not then and not until much later, but my sexual urges were definitely much stronger than with most men. How did I manage to live this enforced celibacy? I was thirteen when my sexuality presented itself and 28 before I finally got married. Fifteen years of sexual frustration. As far as that was concerned I might as well have gone for the priesthood. With that Sacrament I would have had an extra weapon to tame the flames. Once I heard about a fellow who, while masturbating, hit a lightbulb hanging from the ceiling, the bulb shattering on impact. I tried to emulate that feat, missed the bulb but did hit the ceiling. Everyone did it, sex with a woman I mean, but those were rumors, unsubstantiated and never involving people of my own environment. Why wouldn't I do likewise? Of course, idealism played a large role. And free sex also had its shadow sides, or at least so I was told. I doubt it, however, whether I would ever have married Lotte if we first had lived together for at least a year or so. The priorities of the Church were clearly much different from those of its members. Would Christ have meant it to be this way when he appointed Peter as his successor?

In this pregnant though virgin period of engagement I had almost called off the wedding, about half a year before it would take place. Lotte and I were constantly arguing. About just about anything and everything, such as what chairs to buy or wall-to-wall carpeting versus wooden floor. The insidious doubts had some more fundamental reasons too. There was still no indication whatsoever that she loved me in some way. I should have pushed on but what stopped me? Of course I remembered the other time when I had broken off he engagement, two years earlier. And I sharply remembered how miserable I had felt without Lotte. Was it really about 'without Lotte' or rather 'without woman' and about then having to search for another Princess again? I also told myself that it was highly unfair with respect to Lotte to break my promise of marriage. She had invested now some five years in this relation. Foolishness perhaps, but here was again that knight on his white horse attempting to save the maiden. The lessons taught by my mentors were just too permanently engraved on my being. Charles the Magnificent, Carel and Elegast, the times of knightly honor and courteousness, my teacher Netherlands Language had it all beautifully molded together with the adoration for Maria and the notion that we young men were there to protect the maidens. The: "And do not bring us into temptation" from the "Our Father" we took very literally. During our student years we had never met any students who 'were doing it'. We would have known because such things never remain secret. Yet, there were plenty of couples. They all had made this promise to each other and to God.

Had we been ten years younger and had we thus arrived at the University ten years later, we would have found a totally different world. By then the Pill had caught on and just about all students were cohabiting with girlfriend or boyfriend, excepting those who were in a brief in-between stage.

So, we had gotten married. Lotte talked about it in terms of 'giving a good show', a point of view I did not understand. Romantic feelings were still not in her. At least not in any noticeable way. Dressed in tails and with stove pipe hat I would enter a new life; again I became man but that was lost in the noise of the event. Hey! Here I was entering a commitment for life, before the world and before God. In my nervousness I forgot to take off my hat when I entered the church. In fact there was a lot more than show business at hand. On the altar we promised to love each other in good times and bad. The actual words were: "To love and to cherish each other". The word "love" is not powerful enough, probably through over-use. A man may love his wife but he also loves his roses, his soccer, his pint and his dog with little difference in inner experience. "To cherish" is different; it describes an emotion. It is a romantic form of loving. In a marriage 'loving' has to be two-way. But that was exactly not the case with us. Lotte did not love me; not before and certainly not during our marriage. Our marriage was strictly one-way, carried by my love for her only. She was always my princess, my little queen, for whom I built our palace and to whom I dedicated my work, my life, everything. Both in the document of marriage as in the spoken words on the altar Lotte essentially committed perjury, something I have reproached her for bitterly later on.

I even could have let the marriage declared invalid, or at least have applied to the Church for it. The Roman Catholic Church does not recognize divorce but it may declare a marriage nil and void. There are many possible reasons for such a void certification. The best-known of these is, of course, when it can be proven that the marriage has never been consummated, in other words if never sexual intercourse has taken place. However, perjury on the altar might well be construed as the marriage never validly having been conducted and therefore *de facto* never having existed. With Lotte this did never enter her mind. She considered the marriage ceremony as something purely administrative. And also as a license for sex. Something similar we had already earlier experienced during the civil marriage at city hall. That ceremony had been completed in ten minutes flat, after which we had a coffee with rice cake with two friends who had acted as official witnesses. Lotte was well aware of her lie in the church; she considered that of no importance. For her this was something like a white lie, of which even St Augustine had said that they were allowed. With me it was a very different matter. I was also aware of Lotte's lies and deceit. Worse, I even encouraged her to do it. *Force majeure.* If not, there could be no marriage at all and what then? An enforced lie, like telling the Germans that there were no Jews hidden in the attic, the kind of lie that St. Augustine would also condone and even recommend.

Again we have to go back a few years.

XXIX

Enigma

The *Ultra* secret was not just some big secret. Those who are familiar with the history of the second world war will recognize it as the code word for the German Enigma encoding machine. More precisely the extreme secret that the Allies had been able to crack the Enigma codes. They even had a real Enigma machine in their possession without the Germans even suspecting this. And in this way the Allies could listen in on the orders from the *Wehrmacht* headquarters in Berlin about major moves of Army units. They also knew when the feared U-boats would leave harbor and to which coordinates they would be sailing. Usually it concerned high-level orders and that constituted a limitation. The precise complementation was usually left to the local commanders and these did not usually have Enigma machines and who for their communication with units used lower level codes. On that lower level the Allies then had to guess and use additional information from other sources. Furthermore the Enigma codes were often changed and then the Math eggheads in Bletchley Park had to strain again to crack the new code. A war of nerves in other words. However, what did the Allies do with the Enigma information? Only a handful of persons had access to the *Ultra* secrets and Winston Churchill was one of them. That did lead to terrible problems of conscience. For example, at a certain moment he knew that Liverpool would be the next target for the German *Luftwaffe.* He could have concentrated the entire RAF fighter fleet around Liverpool. If he had done so, the Germans would have smelled a rat and would have realized that their beloved secret was out and they would have taken appropriate counter measures. There were higher matters of import and Churchill went to sleep without warning Liverpool.

With Lotte too I was continually confronted with an enigmatic problem. Often enough she was shouting and yelling for hours on end without saying anything; in itself quite an art. There were so many questions, that only she could answer. However, on all questions of any essence, she remained silent and kept remaining silent without ever giving any *clou*. Why did she marry me without loving me and later on actually started hating me? Why did she actually hate all men? She was not even a feminist, of the kind like Germaine Greer, because she did not like women either. She might have said: "Gus, I don't love you, I don't think I will ever love a man. I don't know why that is so, but it is true. I like to be married because of the status, and indeed I like to have children because I like to develop myself as a woman." I probably would have accepted that. It would have been honest and therefore I would have been less of a prisoner, not so much a prisoner of Lotte but rather of my love for her. She said nothing and could never be induced to clarify matters.

Why did she start to hate me so much? All that time this remained totally unclear; her daily returning enigma. I know that she had a very devoted husband in me. Who tried his best to stimulate the development of her abilities. I even took her into my research team. I let her follow computer training. In the end she too was teaching a few Sorbonne colleagues in the finer points of these computer programs. If she had just followed my advice she would certainly have obtained a permanent University appointment. The times were on her side. Universities, though long time male bastions, began to attract an increasing number of female staff. Temporary appointments were converted into permanent ones. This process also took place at our University. One after the other all these women on temporary appointments acquired permanent ones, at least if they so desired. The solutions were all different, cut to the special situation of each person. The only exception was Lotte who refused to even send in an open application to declare her intentions and wishes. Without such a letter the Head of the Math Department was powerless to do anything for her. First complaining that she was discriminated and then, when the opportunity arose, refusing to take it, and finally stepping back entirely. Her reproaches that I had destroyed her life never diminished. Who can see through this enigma? Who can understand her extreme jealousy? Any a bit normal woman would have said: "Gus I know that I cannot give the warmth, that goes with your personality. I am happy with all you have given me and therefore ….". No, Gus needed to be totally destroyed. Lotte's jealousy knew no bounds. It was not only about my contacts with other women.

She became just as jealous with my male friends. At a certain point none of them was any longer welcome in our home. Lotte just chased them away. Her commentary was: "No, your discussions are far too interesting". She was equally jealous about my singing voice. Just less than a year before our divorce I gave her a book of Schubert songs, for piano and baritone. With my clear intention that we would do something musical together. She never even opened the book; I have never seen it again. When I fell ill, I took to my long-forgotten stamp collection. She became so jealous about that collection that she had the album already in her hands planning to tear it to shreds. She only stopped when I mentioned to her that these stamps had monetary value. She was also jealous about my love of music. At a certain point I was already getting better and for my birthday I got a portable radio with cassette and CD player from my children. Lotte got so jealous that she forbade me to use the thing. Only after she got a similar present from her children six months later (ha, had I ever been devious in suggesting this to my children!) she relented. After which she forbade me to play Maria Callas in her famous "Norma" arias. Her jealousy with regard to my academic successes I have mentioned earlier; that particular jealousy served to destroy even my academic and scientific career. All these jealousy activities did not make her any happier. They actually enhanced her feelings of discomfort. The jealousy was not productive and yet she persisted in it. If anyone understands this enigma he/she has my agreement to tell about it, but I certainly did not understand it, all these years. It felt like I was missing the key to the code.

There is only one explanation which fits all facts. As is not rare at all with very difficult problems, the solution is very simple and easy to find. In all its simplicity the solution was also absurd but that too fitted the absurdity of Lotte's behavior. The essence of absurdity is that it lies beyond the realm of understanding, because it is something that one has never experienced, because it does not jibe with other facts of life and because initially it appears to be impossible. Therefore it borders on the surrealistic. It took until about ten years after my divorce before the understanding began to break through. With more stability in my life came the clarity which allowed me to think the unthinkable. Just as in scientific work where lateral jumps from one line of thought to another lead to breakthroughs, here too there was this spark. A spark that quickly was extinguished, only to come back again. And next to be pushed out again: "This cannot be, this is impossible, this is contrary to everything I know, this is self-contradictory". And yet it came back, hesitatingly knocking on a door that refused to open, until I finally understood that this illogic had its own logic: "Gus, I hate you so much because you love me so much".

Words that were never spoken by Lotte, which nevertheless touched the heart of the problem. Lotte hated me because I loved her so much. Every time I showed her my love in words, gestures or behavior, she hated me for it. The more love she received from me and the longer it lasted the deeper and all-embracing her hate became. Why? Because she felt that love every time, and at the same time was unable to answer it. Each and every time she felt her own shortcoming. Every expression of my love for her reminded her of her own inability to love. Logical too that she was unable to talk about it.

"I hate you because of your loving me". How could she possibly say this? To me, to her children, to her family. "That is why I could not divorce you, that is why you had go away from me nevertheless, away and out of my life. When you did not leave voluntarily in spite of all the pestering and you still were there, I had to kill you, whatever the consequences of such a murder. Your love would only disappear with your death."

XXX

Breaking Marriage

I had really thought that with the arrival of the first baby everything would change but that had turned out to be a terrible miscalculation. By itself that baby was indeed a splendid baby, but it changed nothing. After two years of marriage the awful feeling began to set in with me that this marriage would perhaps never succeed. For the first time my thoughts turned to divorce. Was it really that hopeless? I tried to find help, outside help, but Lotte would not hear of it. And without her collaboration nothing would change. I tried this for at least twenty long years, only to obtain the same negative commentary. The reasons for her rejection sometimes varied in emphasis, but it all came down to four themes:

"Yes, I know what you want. You want to have me locked up in an asylum". This one I heard from early times onward in various variants. That was not my plan at all; I wanted her at home and happy. It is remarkable though, that Lotte kept repeating this so often. Obviously this scenario lived within her, the fear of being institutionalized, just like her mother. She was smart enough to know that indeed there was something wrong with her psyche.

"There is absolutely nothing wrong with our marriage". "Well Lotte, if that is so, why then are we arguing all the time and why are you then so unhappy?" But these two questions she never answered. To make one thing clear, our arguing was always about our marriage and never about money and only rarely about our children.

"There is nothing wrong with our marriage that we cannot repair ourselves". "Then how come, Lotte, that we are always arguing about the same points without ever coming to solutions?" Matters such as Lotte's refusal to write a letter of application to the Math Department. Or my refusal to give up my research. Or Lotte' opinion that all men are Male Chauvinist Pigs, no one exempted. Or Lotte's accusation that I was standing in the way of her development *et cetera*.

"There is nothing wrong with me; it is all your fault". "OK, Lotte, if that is so then why is it then that you cannot tell me what I have done wrong, because now you leave me in the dark. The more reason to engage a relation counsellor. You tell him all the things I am doing wrong and then he may translate that to me, so that I will know what I am doing wrong and how to change things."
 Nope, njet, nada, nichts, nothing, zero, zilch.

Was really nothing right in this marriage? Oh, yes, absolutely; there were plenty of beautiful moments. We got one, two, three beautiful children, girls all three and this *Dreimädelhaus* was the joy of my life. I thought it really terrific to be a father and I took care that they got quality time from me, even though my work and career were of consuming interest too. I had a splendid home, built according to my own design; ultimately it had five bedrooms and four bathrooms. The living room had a cathedral ceiling with a free standing fireplace at the high end. The kitchen was super; every drawer or knob had been thought out. At least twice a day I was present at the building site to consult with the various contractors. The home had unique aspects such as a bar in the living room; in Canada (barely escaped from prohibition) this was unthinkable. Separate toilets were also a novelty in North America where everybody asks for the bathroom. The garden was also very special. In the semi-desert climate with temperatures going from -40 to +40, I created a flower garden that was widely admired and even photographed. My University work also went well; I was quickly accepted and admired for my knowledge and my energy. In no time flat I was elected in all kinds of important committees. Lotte showed barely any interest in all this, not even for the magnificent kitchen I had designed for her. Her talents were soon discovered, though. She began teaching Math at the University on the freshmen level. No problems here with order in the classroom and therefore this went very smoothly. We had therefore all kinds of reasons for both of us to feel very happy. Believe it or not; within the University world we were considered to be a model couple.

XXXI

Niels Stensen

How had we ended up in Canada? The direct reason for this were the anti-Catholic sentiments which were still rife in the Netherlands *anno* 1963. I beg your pardon? Yes, you are reading correctly. The Concord between the Vatican and the Netherlands was already 110 years old. Once more one could legally be a Catholic. Hundreds of Catholic churches had been built since then. Catholics could be civil servants even! There was a Catholic University and there was 'special education' meaning Catholic primary and secondary schools. However, appearances may deceive. Some professions were still virtually closed for Catholics. There were still very few Catholic University professors. At the Leyden University their number was even zero. One apparent exception; there was a Chair for Thomistic philosophy. This was a 'special' Chair and therefore not part of the Leyden University itself. This Chair was paid for by the Catholic Church. This did not really undermine the long-held policy of 'no Catholic professors'; this one toleration in fact emphasized the *de facto* discrimination. There was also little or no Catholic lower staff at the Universities. Why would you want to become a Scientific Officer (a civil service rank) if you knew beforehand that you would never be considered for higher academic positions?

That same University of Leyden appointed a Catholic professor some 400 years ago. This man from Denmark called Nils Stensen (also known as Niels Steensen) was a world-famous scientist; the founder of such disciplines like Biology, Biochemistry, Geology, Mineralogy to name a few. At one time he had been ordained as a priest and had even his first purple Bishop's stripes. However, for that appointment in Leyden he had gladly and *pro forma* become a Calvinist. In those days one was sometimes easygoing in these matters. Willem of Orange, *nota bene* the founder of Leyden University, had done the same or worse. First he was a Lutheran, then converted to Catholicism and finally Calvinist. He always knew from which direction the wind was blowing.

A bold plan was designed, concocted by a few well-known and prominent Dutch Catholics. First Catholic cadre had to be developed in order to create a pool of young people who were in principle of Professor quality. In order to get there, promising young academics had to be sent abroad for high-level training. That plan would cost much money. There was always one thing Catholics were allowed to do and that was to be in business. As a result there were in the Netherlands a number of very rich Catholic business families. Well known examples are V&D, C&A and many more. The initiators first visited the Brenninkmeijer family, owners of the C&A chain. They immediately adopted the idea and provided an initial sum of fl.50,000.00. That was enough to send the first grantees abroad in 1959. They planned to approach more wealthy people but this turned out to be not needed. The Brenninkmeijer family to the present day has footed the entire bill. When recently the Niels Stensen Foundation (the instrument name of this activity) celebrated its 50st birthday it turned out that already more than 300 grantees had been sent abroad.

In the meantime I had completed my full doctorate. While I was looking for a suitable industrial position, I was made aware of the Niels Stensen Foundation. I applied and indeed was awarded a very substantial grant for me and my family. My laboratory of choice was the National Research Council in Ottawa, Canada, which had a world reputation at the time. Two delightful years long we spent in that beautiful country, while I tried to suck up the fine art of doing significant scientific research. Then back to the Netherlands to our home, to the job that had been kept open for me. Very shortly after our return I heard that there was a proposal in the works to promote me to lector, the step-up rank to a full professorate. Hurrah, the Niels Stensen system had worked. I would get a scientific career at a Netherlands University.

Alas, alas. A few months later I was told that the promotion proposal had not been accepted. I was told that our Faculty did not want any lectors, only full professors and for the latter I was rather young. Bloody nonsense, because at all Universities there were lectors and even some at other Faculties at our own University.

Indeed shortly after this incident, even our own Faculty appointed a first lector. I had not awaited this. I was disappointed and angry, but not defeated. I knew my value and then the Gods came to give me a helping hand.

XXXII

The Loge and Emigration

Where is this fear of Catholicism coming from? Why is it so persistent? In the sixteenth century the war against Spain had become a war for freedom. Not only political freedom because blockades and the like had always been easy to circumvent. The trading always went on. No, in particular it had been a war for religious freedom. At least that was always stated. However, barely had the Spaniards been defeated or the religious intolerance set in. The Netherlands Reformed Church became practically the official State religion. Not only was Catholicism forbidden, the Remonstrants, the Lutherans, the Baptists, they all were persecuted. Suddenly there was no freedom of religion at all. Is this a reason for the continuing anti-Catholicism? Those irrepressible Catholics who through the Catholic State Party (later the Catholic People's Party) were exerting a major influence on life in the Netherlands. Was it fear or shame or outright jealousy? If you ask students, the University of Maastricht (in the deep Catholic South) is presently the best University in the Netherlands, followed by the University of Brabant as an honorable second. The world-famous University of Leyden is just nowhere. The Province of North Brabant is presently the most productive Province of all, outclassing South Holland with its Rotterdam harbor. Therefore plain jealousy? Or shame because all the stolen property of the Roman Catholic Church and her servants?

Perhaps the problem lies on a much deeper level. Perhaps it is not so much anti-Catholicism but rather an act of continuously-felt Calvinist impotence. If you take cognizance of the pure Calvinist doctrine you cannot help but be impressed. It is all deeply religious, very pure and elevated. Yes, in particular a high ethical level, with God as the highest and sole guideline in our human lives. Nothing is allowed between us and Him; only by the direct contact between us as a human being and Him the pure truth could be found. Because of this doctrine Calvin eventually rejected the priesthood as intermediary between man and God. And hence too his rejection of the Sacraments. All grace could only come from God himself. The problem with this Calvinism is that one has to be endowed with considerable intellectual powers in order to be able to embrace it. For 95% of mankind this is simply too difficult. You cannot stop those millions of women who approach Maria in their prayers, asking her for intercession, because her Son is too far away and too high anyway. And then the Confession! By doing away with the Confession the baby was really thrown out along with the bathing water. Now the father confessor has been replaced by an army of tens of thousands psychiatrists, psychologists and psycho therapists to help all these people with their existential fears. Is that system any better?

"Ah, you Catholics, you believe your sins will be forgiven just by going into that confessional box with a priest". Heard many times, even very recently from a Netherlands Reformed woman, in 2010. How on earth is it possible? Where had she gotten that from? "From the minister during catechization lessons". "Did your minister also tell you that there are three major conditions for a valid confession? Contrition, confession and reparation. Contrition or remorse not just because you got caught, no, because what you did was an insult to God. That also includes a very solid and firm undertaking to never commit that sin again. Confession? Yes, absolutely. Before a priest, a minister of the cloth or another guidance person or even in public, in such a way that God can hear you. The truth, the whole truth, nothing but the truth. Surely also reparation. Return the stolen goods, go to the person you insulted and say sorry, correct injustice you perpetrated. Sometimes it is difficult or even impossible to undo your error; in that case your father confessor will help to find an alternative. Never forget though, that only God can forgive. The priest is only an intermediary, his absolution is conditional and totally void if you cheat on the process. And did your minister tell you all that during the catechization?" "No" said the woman, rather taken aback. She had no idea how difficult and demanding a good confession may be.

Ha, that delightful feeling of freedom of liberation after Confession, after that *absolve te* from the priest, when you feel, you know, that you are friends again with God. Then you are dancing through life again!

We Catholics are good sinners. Not that we are leading a loose life. No, because we know that we have a loving Father, who has created us and who therefore knows we will fail once and a while and who therefore may forgive us when we ask for it. And that is precisely where it chafes with the Calvinists. Typically he does not dare to admit to his errors and sins because he has no means of getting rid of the burden of those sins. Will God ever forgive him? He will never know and he can never be sure. And that is why the typical Calvinist takes refuge in the denial of his sins. Slave trader? Ah, you surely don't believe that those blackies are real humans, created to His likeness, do you? Persecute local people to enrich yourself by it? Ah, it is self-evident that God has appointed us white people to rule over these dumb creatures; they cannot possibly govern themselves. Persecute Catholics? Of course! Because they are servants of a false God, worshipping sculptures. Stolen property? Oh, these people said we could have it all. The hypocrisy of the present-day Calvinist world knows no bounds. Once a friend came to me totally confused and upset. He had visited the prostitutes and now he was extremely sorry and contrite. Well, I had heard that before. Xaviera Hollander, the famous *Madame* with Dutch roots, writes in the introduction of her auto-biography that men from Holland are the world's worst lovers. She writes: "At first they don't want to do it, and after they have done it finally, then they instantly begin to wail that they so sorry". (Note, by the way, that she used the word 'Holland', not 'the Netherlands') My dear friend actually came up with an ingenious solution. When I saw him again, his problem and his regrets were totally gone. He said: "You know, I really did not have any intercourse with that whore. I was wearing a condom and only the outside of that condom was in contact with the vagina of that whore and I was inside". You really have to be a Calvinist to come up with that kind of denial.

XXXIII

Hypocritical Pharisee

Around that same time I came in contact with a remarkable confluence of anti-Papism, jealousy and Calvinist hypocrisy. The PD (= place of delict) was The Hague, always a bulwark of religion-related hypocrisy, stirred up by the Freemason Loge. At the time I was a volunteer at a Walk-in Center. Visitors were offered a cup of coffee or tea and a comfortable chair, so that usually a homey atmosphere prevailed. The volunteers were always available for a talk. The special thing was that this was an ecumenical enterprise with the costs being carried by all Churches and other ideological organizations in the city. One of the initiators was a Catholic priest; unfortunately he retired just at the moment I arrived there. I liked doing this kind of work and as a rule I had a very good relation with the visitors. Often these were people from the underdog fringe of society. There were the homeless, psychotics, junkies, and also ordinary people who had been dealt harshly by life. They all had a story to tell, their life story. From my colleagues I also often got positive feedback. Suddenly I was called in by the chairwoman of a committee who informed me abruptly: "Gus, we have decided to fire you". That went as follows:

"Gus you have behaved improperly by kissing a woman in this place". Yes, that was totally true. That was Gesele, a Flemish lady whom I knew from another organization. She was a volunteer too, accompanying a woman to our place, where we happened to meet each other. It would have been an insult if I had not kissed her on the cheek while greeting her. I reminded my interrogators, that a little while earlier one of our volunteers had embraced a visitor, and waltzed around with him for at least ten minutes. I had wondered whether that was indeed proper. At the time I was told that this particular visitor needed motherly love and that it therefore was allowed. Where was this rule stated and written down? Nowhere, of course. And this other volunteer then, recently decorated by the Queen for all her good work in our Home, whom I recently had seen totally naked, with freshly shaven pubic area, on the public beach of Kijkduin (near the Hague), was that not improper behavior? No reply.

"Gus, you have started a discussion amongst the visitors concerning the fact that during a general cleaning of the aquarium all the fish had been washed away through the toilet". Totally true. For myself I thought this an unnecessary cruelty relative to these animals. However, I wanted to find out what our visitors were thinking about it. After all, this was their living room and their aquarium. In the end I got a very interesting discussion going, with many pros and contras. And what was wrong with that, I asked? Well, implicitly a criticism on the leadership, whomever they were. I had carefully not voiced my own opinion. A good discussion amongst the visitors was that not one of our goals? Again angry looks.

"Gus, you have brought one of your colleagues almost to a nervous breakdown." Well, that must have been Jeanne. She had been begging me for months to come to her home, in particular so that I could have a discussion with her husband, a retired minister of the cloth. I had consistently refused that; in the end I had agreed to have a talk with herself. Jeanne had been made responsible for the selection of new volunteers. My first question was, of course, what criteria she used for this selection. It turned out that she had none. Also the advisory Board had never considered it necessary to develop such criteria. And so it went on and on, until she admitted that she clearly had done everything wrong. I comforted her by saying that she should never have been thrown into such a responsible job without any preparation. Jeanne got what she asked for, so what was there to reproach me for?

"Gus, you have insulted another volunteer and you have called her a cheat". That must have been Christine. This woman calls herself a Medium and a Magnetizer. Being a physicist I must say that by any definition she is a conwoman. She never should have become a volunteer in our group working with our very vulnerable clients. Furthermore she had with a hammer put a dent in a door of her own car and next accused me of having caused the damage. Would I please contact my insurance company? She had explained that this is the way it works in the Netherlands. If there is a little scratch too small for repairs, then you make it a little worse in order to get it repaired and charged to the Insurance. I had indeed indicated to Christine that I never collaborate in such malpractices. I asked if it was expected of me as a volunteer to commit such fraud? More angry looks.

"Gus you have refused to take part in the formation weekends. These are compulsory, you know". Where was this stated, I asked. Nowhere. Furthermore it seems to me that you can never make this compulsory to volunteers. There was a reason why I did not take part in these weekends. You have to play role games. That is very good for new, inexperienced people but with my more than fifty years in the education field, with all kinds of leading functions, it appeared to me that I did not need these. In addition, I was afraid that, while playing these roles, I would start speaking unwelcome truths and that seemed not very wise. I had kept my mouth shut regarding doubtful practices and situations for several years, so why take then such risks.

So it went on. A couple of persons had questioned many people in our organization about me and carefully collected accusatory items against me. In secret, without letting me know anything. I suspect they had taken their cue from Florian Henckel's movie: "*Das Leben der Anderen*" about the East-German *Stasi* methods in the former DDR. A secret witch hunt, without reference to any existing rules or laws, without any right to countermand or defend, without any rights for appeal, without confrontation with the accusing persons, without possibility to ask questions, without right to legal counsel.

For the first time in its 25 years of existence a volunteer had been dismissed! What on earth could be behind this?

A partial answer became clear within a few days. Two more colleagues had been similarly dismissed. The common denominator? All three were Catholics! One was a nun who already for many years had been working as a volunteer in this Center. She was told to resign because her work supposedly had been no good. Never anybody had told her this before. The third one was a new addition to our staff, who had had lots of experience in the field of human contacts. He was pestered by one of the leaders of this witch hunt to an extend that he resigned. At that point there were only two Catholics left amongst the sixty-odd volunteers we had. Other contributing factors may have been jealousy and fear. Fear in particular for my evident intellectual gifts, jealousy because I did a very good job.

Perhaps we should just feel sorry for these Calvinists. They are wretched people, really. The best amongst them do really seek God. He seems to be so far away to them, that they fail to see that He is also very nearby. Their tortured uncertainty I have been able to observe many times from close-up. Their struggle, not being able, not daring to accept total truth, saddened me often. If, in addition, they also believe in predestination, then they suffer under a system of refined cruelty, that makes even the strongest break down. An exquisite form of cruelty indeed far outpacing those of the Marquis de Sade. They seem to totally forget the message of love brought by God's Son to the people of this earth, in a language of this earth, in an earthy manner understandable by all.

It is all so unnecessary if they, with the Catholics, could believe that God is Goodness and Love. The Calvinists see God rather like a very severe punishing God whom you better not get too close to. Their attempts to hide their sinning "I" look very pathetic; He is Almighty and Allseeing isn't He? In the practice of the daily life it is rather difficult to deal with these people in a normal fashion. All lesser aspects of the total truth have to stay outside the discussion. Nothing is so shameful like being confronted with these negative aspects. Imagine that He would hear it!

XXXIV

Canada the first Time Around

In this manner Lotte and I spent two wonderful years in that splendid country called Canada. We learned to ski at a very large ski center, only a few miles away from our home. We also made some short and longer camping trips. This was entirely new for Lotte but I have to say that she quickly became an expert camper who was really thinking ahead. For example, she made a very handy bag for all the cutlery and she learned to cook on a primitive gasoline burner. She also became expert in the routine of setting up and breaking down our tent. She also became pregnant of Astrid, our second child. Actually, that had already happened on the boat; what else is there to do during ten days at sea? Play more bridge? What else, man! Well, frankly speaking, a bit of love or even a bit more affinity and kindness would have worked miracles with me. Bitter feelings crept into my heart. Sometimes this feeling was so hurtful that I really began to think of death as a sweet escape device.

That second child was born in Ottawa; as it happened in the same suite where then Princess Juliana had born her daughter Margriet some twenty years earlier. Soon therefore another baby was crawling through our home; it appeared to be a cry-baby. In her pen she began to cry as soon as she saw Lotte or me. Lotte thought that perhaps her breast feeding was not enough so that the baby was plain hungry all the time. However, the regular weigh-ins at the health center indicated that the weight of the baby was normal or just above it. When I got home and I picked Astrid up from her pen, then she immediately fell silent. Any mother would have understood that; the child just wanted to be cuddled. However, that was something Lotte never did.

Towards the end of our stay we made a very long camping trip through the USA and back through the Canadian Rocky Mountains. We saw all the famous sights: the Golden Gate, the Sequoia trees, Death Valley and the Grand Canyon. There again that feeling came over me; one little step forward and it would be all over. The infinite beauty of the landscape next to the denial of life itself. And why would Lotte then be allowed to live on? She, who did not care at all about beauty; she, who denied love. With a sigh I turned away from the seductive abyss, only to look straight into the expecting eyes of the toddler looking at her daddy.

XXXV

Ma's Reincarnation

We had returned to the Netherlands and promptly experienced problems with the wet climate, with Ma and with the Dutch science world. In principle we had decided to move again, in fact back to Canada, this time permanently as emigrants. In the meantime we had three children; during the boat trip back across the ocean Lotte had again proven fertile. Mieke was our third daughter. Years later, when she congratulated me on Father's Day I sent her a limerick:

On the great ship she was conceived at leisure
Nine months later she was born as our third treasure
Now she wants to thank me on this Father's Day
For being her Dad, but to her I say
Don't thank me; it was just my pleasure

In the meantime I had accepted a position as tenured Associate Professor at a brand new Canadian University. It is always very interesting to start and build something new and I threw myself with full energy into my new job. We had attempted to associate ourselves with the Catholic parish to which we belonged geographically speaking, but this had turned out to be a disappointment. The children went to the parish schools and we attended Sunday Mass in that church. The parish priest made a very poor impression though. When, after a full year, he still did not recognize me and greeted me at the door with: "Hello stranger", I had seen enough. Next we sought and found good company in the non-geographical French-language parish of *St. Jean Batiste;* in the end this turned out to be a golden decision. Fact is that our children were already going to the bilingual French-English school. Lotte and I took some French courses to freshen up our school French. During an international Conference I had met some French colleagues who were doing research closely related to mine. Slowly a nice little plan evolved. My first sabbatical came into view. Would it not be nice to spend that sabbatical in France?

In the meantime we also befriended also other 'European' colleagues (and their families) at this University. To get this straight: in Canada 'European' means the continent on the other side of the Channel, entirely in the tradition of the London Times: "Fog over the Channel, Continent isolated". Our Old-to-New Year parties were famous, if not infamous. The design of our home was eminently suitable for parties. We could easily have fifty guests without getting overcrowded.

Everything seemed to move smoothly, until that moment that I had told Lotte that at the University a proposal was in the works to make me a Full Professor. This had led to an outburst from her side, an explosion of long kept-in anger: "When was her time to become a Full Professor?" When would her chance come? Everything had gone toward the development of my career and now I got all the honor and she got nothing. She was just 'the wife of' professor van der Molenschot.

At first sight there might seem some truth to her sentiments; nevertheless her outburst hit me straight in the stomach. I thought her reproaches highly unfair and in due time I replied to her with several arguments.

When Lotte completed her Math doctoral we held a mighty garden party. We announced that there would be a major book burning and that furthermore the wine cellar had to be emptied. At that occasion Lotte declared loudly that from that moment onwards she would concentrate on making babies and confiture (the latter to symbolize het domestic intentions). Next she indeed burned all her math books and even those course notes she had worked on so assiduously together with her friend Elly. Not really the behavior of someone planning an academic career. Of course we had talked extensively about this division of tasks even long before we got married. There is no way to push back these babies where they came from once they were born. If Lotte now wanted to change her opinion, she should show considerably more than just anger.

We were in the sixties. In that time it was quite normal that women first concentrated on getting children and then later would participate (again) in outside work process. The faculty wives at our University almost all had a University degree but most were quite content with their status. Some of them were teaching part time at the University as instructor on a course by course base. Lotte did more than most. She had developed an interest in computers. I had even sent her to the US for a course in applied computer science. She did most of the computer calculations for my research. Not only did I pay her for this whenever I had the funds, but she also co-authored some of the publications. Her name would have been on a lot more publications if my illness had not interrupted the work. Now there are only a few such papers. However, all this was a lot more than any other wife-of-professor could show. In essence we followed the mores of the time while at the same time we were at the leading edge in women emancipation.

Lotte had never shown any interest in Mathematics as a scientific discipline. She was not a member of any Mathematics organization, she never read any published Math papers and she never attended any of the weekly seminars that the Math Department organized. She never worked on any Mathematics project developing something novel. She never showed any initiative to obtain a full doctorate. The latter was a prerequisite for any professor appointment. She had plenty of time for it. Her income from teaching we did not really need and we had enough money to hire a housekeeper.

Lotte never replied to these points. She felt done in and she felt that a professorate should just be given to her. This all hit me heavily. It was bad enough that she did not love me, but now she appeared to blame me for it. I had tried so hard to make her happy, never mind that my possibilities were also limited. I strongly suspected that she really did not want help. The last thing she wanted was that her demands would be fulfilled. All she wanted was to be unhappy so that she would have reason to complain. She was admired by many people around for what she could do and in fact did. She had three fantastic children and a doting and loving husband (and indeed everyone knew that to be true). She took part in high-level scientific work. However, she reacted by finding something she did NOT have, something she was absolutely not entitled to but which could serve to feed her unhappiness. In short: Lotte had created a reincarnation of Ma. Instead of enjoying our upcoming stay in France a dirty mood pervaded our home. I felt literally as if somebody had kicked me in the crotch. Lotte had hit me in my manhood. I had made a complete woman of her and as thanks for all my love I was now thrown out as garbage. No, that is not quite right. I had to stay on of course, as target.

XXXVI

The Ultimatum

If you would think that Lotte would leave it at that, then you are sadly mistaken. Well, in effect there was enough to do concerning that stay in France. Seeing family, making a grandiose camping trip through France with the brand new Volvo, French language lessons at the *Institut Catholique,* finding schools for the children, new French acquaintances, the lot. Hard on the return to Canada the attack was renewed. The original plan had already been anti-Gus and now she continued on that theme. Gus was the cause, the reason that she had not been able to develop herself. He was the reason that she would not get the chances that he so richly gave himself. This he had achieved amongst others by saddling her with three children plus the responsibility for running the house keeping. Now the attack intensified.

She put it directly to Gus that he should stop his scientific work and that he should also cease his organizational work for the University. He would be allowed to do his teaching provided he would be home by 12:30. Then he would clean the house, make the beds, peel the potatoes and cook the dinner and next put the children to bed after which he would do the laundry, iron it all and prepare the list for his shopping trip to the Superstore. In the meantime Lotte would prepare herself for the Full Professorate.

Please read the above once more and then a few more times. Perhaps one can imagine that someone in an angry outburst says something like it, but with Lotte it was totally different. It was icy, cold and calculating, it was said in a calm voice and repeated many times during that year. Later again for months on end. What kind of woman, what kind of wife would do such a thing to a husband? She had only one argument: it was now her turn. She never made it clear why my career would have to be sacrificed for it. She never said that I should resign, to the contrary. The idea was that I would still pull my full salary as Full Professor, while stopping all but some undergraduate classes. To me that constituted fraud, but Lotte remained deaf to any such points. How could I possibly receive a fat salary and not work for it? For sure the Head of the Chemistry Department would take exception to it; not only would he protest; in the end it would mean a dishonorable discharge. "They won't dare to do that to you", Lotte maintained, but I was sure I would be fired.

Why could she never give a meaningful kiss or any other affective gesture? The children never got a kiss either. I cannot say that she hated her children; she certainly did not love them either. Why could she enjoy me in bed without ever coming close or letting me come close to her? Why is it that she could not talk about these matters either? Not even with a psychiatrist or other professional, although she knew full well that she had psychic problems? One particular fear sometimes surfaced. When I suggested once more to seek help she always had a ready reply: "Yes, I know what you want. You want to see me locked up in an institution". The periods that Ma had been taken into a psychiatric hospital ward were never from her mind. Not even when she had agreed to marry me. She had added that she agreed to marry me but that she did not love me. And then she had added one more condition: "You must promise me, Gus, that you will never let me being locked up". I had immediately understood what she meant and why. I promised her solemnly. A promise that later I kept constantly before my eyes, when it became relevant. A promise that I have kept, even when I had to pay a very high price for it.

Slowly there came some reactions from Lotte, but very few and not very useful, because they were always totally negative. For example regarding our prenuptial agreement. She would say: "Yes, perhaps I then thought that way but now I think this way". There is that kind of kooky argument. I did not reply in kind. Suppose I had said that I at one time promised to support a family but that now I was thinking differently? I can well imagine how Lotte would react to such an approach.

I kept hammering away at the weakest point of Lotte's reasoning. There was much she could do without first destroying my career. To start with, she might begin attending the Math Seminars that were conducted weekly. And she might do some investigation into the possibilities to get a full doctorate degree. "Never", was the reply to all these suggestions. No, first I had to stop working and come home. How was I to do that?

"Tell your Head that you are stopping".

"What about my Masters an PhD students then?"

"Tell them too that you are stopping".

"I then very likely will be fired".

"They won't dare to do that".

I was not so sure. In fact I was pretty sure that firing would be the result. It would not have been the first one on this Campus. Our Department in particular had a tremendous reputation. About half the Masters and PhD theses on this Campus came from this one Department. Such a reputation does not happen by itself. It was the result of very hard work by all colleagues. To carry out Lotte's plan would be construed as refusal to work.

How precisely Lotte intended to start her career was never specified by her. She would not reveal any detail except by saying what she NOT would do. The suggestion, for example, that she would enter a PhD program was a good example. She literally blew her lid in a massive explosion. Her reaction was simple:

"No, they have to take me the way I am".

"In any case you will have to write a letter of application to the Head of the Math Department. You could say that after the many years of contract work a position would be in order, if only on the level of Assistant Professor".

"Absolutely not", was her reply, "I won't write a letter. They know where I live".

"Listen Lotte, you surely realize that you are putting your Head in an impossible position. How can he go to bat for you if he does not even know what it is that you want? He has to go to the Dean of the Faculty with a proposal. How can he do that without any supporting documentation, not even a letter from you indicating what you want? Plus that there has to be an up-dated CV where you can mention also all your research work, next to your teaching experience".

Nyet, nada, nothing, zilch, null, no, no, no.

In the early years of this University there had been a few faculty members without a PhD; they did have a Masters as highest diploma. These people had received an appointment as Assistant Professor. In a few Departments, notably Computer Science and Business Administration this had been done because it had proven impossible to otherwise attract new faculty members. For a few others it had been done under a so-called Grandfather's clause; this new University had been created partly out of a pre-University College. Understandably the teaching staff of this College had to be incorporated into the University in a decent fashion.

Now, when we arrived, the situation was fundamentally different. The University had become very conservative in regard to appointing faculty in positions which could lead to tenure, *i.e.* an appointment for life. The Faculty of Science, where Mathematics resorted under had become very strict in this matter. If Lotte desired a permanent position she would have to present a career plan. However, Lotte remained adamant; no letter of application, no CV, no career plan. So what choice was there for the head of the Math Department? He was perfectly willing and sympathetic but under these circumstances he could do nothing for Lotte. In fact he just had been forced to give up one faculty member under an enforced budget cut. At that moment there was absolutely no maneuvering space. Lotte was fully aware of all this. She was told so by the Head of the Math Department and from me she got the same story in even greater detail.

In spite of his Lotte kept pressing her demand. I would have to give up my career and in fact immediately. In hindsight I find it remarkable, unbelievable even, that for a while I seriously considered doing what she asked. It caused much pain and anguish. Of course I wanted to help Lotte in any way possible; now she asked me the impossible. It was technically not possible on punishment of total ruin of our core family. Personally I could not bring myself to it either. Because of the fraud, because of the betrayal of my various duties, because of the love for my job and mostly because of my total non-understanding of this plan. Suppose I would give in. I felt sure that I would then be fired. Would the University then next hire Lotte? A person who refused to apply, who refused to provide a CV and a career plan?

Lotte was all but stupid. The whole point of her demand was of course that it could never succeed. She knew that full well and that is exactly why she formulated it that way. Women are from Venus and Men are from Mars. Forever men are falling into that trap. Females are not impressed when their demands are met. In fact they often resent this because then their reasons for complaining are taken away. More than anything else women want to be listened to. Well that I had done for many years and I had at the same time converted that into positive items. To no avail.

Anyone would have concluded long before that Lotte's goal was to destroy me by hitting me where my second largest love was, my second greatest devotion and joy in life. Professor Gus had to be destroyed, that was evident, considering Lotte's behavior, wasn't it? It is perhaps strange that I drew that conclusion only much later, in fact only many years later. Years after the divorce had become a fact. Then what else? Lotte's systematic, never altering, never wavering, never any doubts or moderation showing behavior had an alternate explanation. An explanation that wasn't even in contradiction with the most obvious one, but indeed much more encroaching. Lotte was psychotic, very ill in fact, and for me that was a major reason to keep accepting her weird behavior. She could not help it, could she? One way to describe her psychosis is by the word 'victimitis', the tendency to always see oneself as a victim. Is there really nothing to complain, well, then the patient will fabricate some. It is a technique that always works; just make some impossible demands and your complaints are ready made.

XXXVII

The Compromise

It was around this time that Lotte really began to hate me. Or more properly stated, that she began to voice it. It must have been present latently because now she spitted it out in a vehement fashion, both in intensity and frequency like Old Faithful in Yellowstone Park. With great regularity I now heard her:

"I hate you, I hate you, I hate you".

She did it standing right in front of me, sitting down across of me at the table, laying down in bed, anywhere as soon as we were alone, outside hearing range for anybody. Strangely enough she always did it in English. We had an undertaking of always speaking proper Dutch to each other, carefully avoiding Anglicisms. Any time some tiny error crept in we would politely correct each other, because we wanted to keep our mother language pure. Not now. Whenever Lotte wanted to scold, she did it in English. Psychology anybody?

Initially I did not take this fiery language all too seriously. I thought that she really meant something else, without being able to put her finger on the right spot. Something was bothering her and I happened to be close by. At night, she usually crept up to me and then we made love again, or whatever passed for it. How could you possibly do this with a person if you really hated him? Another enigma. Perhaps she hated herself because she needed me?

Yet, seen from another angle, she must have hated me very deeply, at least at the very moments she made these utterings. I still believe that at these moments she really meant what she said. That I and no-one or nothing else was the reason that she was not a professor. If she indeed believed this then in her mind her husband must have been an awful son-of-a-bitch. The facts, the verifiable facts pointed in a totally different direction, however. It was Lotte who had lost contact with the real world. In periods, Lotte was really schizophrenic. Often she rolled from the one world into another world and then back.

After many months of heated discussions we finally reached an agreement. Hurrah, our system had prevailed. I had been able to convince Lotte that she could have her career without first destroying mine. We were going to build an addition to our home and that would serve for a live-in house keeper who would do all that physical home work that neither of us two wanted to do. We were looking for someone who would also be good with the children and who would be at home when the children arrived from school. After prolonged pushing Lotte finally went along with this plan and for a short while even the old good spirit came over her. She even invested some of her own money into the construction of the addition. What is this, all of a sudden? Lotte with her own money? Even that I had arranged for her. For a long time we had only one bank account, jointly held by us two. In fact I had no money of my own. The savings I once had were spent on buying the building lot for our home. The home we had in the Netherlands had been bought by my money; when I sold it all of a sudden it was our money. In the same way my salary was our money, naturally. However, I had gone much further than that. In order to support Lotte in her search for self-consciousness I had proposed that all the money she earned she could put into a bank account of her own. Of course, the cost for domestic help was charged to our joint account (say, my money). For income tax purposes I could no longer deduct Lotte as a dependent so that was a further loss to our joint account. All that time I had no account in my own name. Naïve? With hindsight, yes, and incredibly so. Our home also stood in both our names. Stupid? Perhaps, because this kind of idealism would cost me very dearly later on.

XXXVIII

Incest

Just when you finally think you are beginning to understand what is happening, a wrench is thrown into the spokes. Something happens that considerably enlarges the enigma. My joy regarding my three children had always been very considerable. You are supposed to love them equally but the one personality is not like the other. Astrid was a bit introvert, perhaps a genetic throwback to her Saxon grandfather on her mother's side. Mieke, our number three, was a typical number three, rather carelessly floating through life, sometimes a clown, then suddenly a rock. Number one was a totally different type. Dark as a Spanish woman, she had something from both grandmothers. Surely she was beautiful, even as a child; something she realized full well herself. She was also Daddy's pet. That is not supposed so to be in any family and when it came down to it I loved all three equally. However, this one crept on daddy's lap till she was sixteen and then we had a nice hug. Both grandmothers I said? Therefore including Ma? Very much so, but that would evolve only over time.

Our marriage was in the danger zone again and for quite a while already. The eldest two had left home, studying at far-away Universities. It came out only in a by-the-way fashion, Lotte mentioning it during a rather intense discussion on a non-related topic. She mentioned that number one daughter, then no more than eleven years old, had come to her mother saying that her father had touched her in a sexual way. Incest! Lotte had not believed her at all, had told me nothing and had next all forgotten about it. Just as well, since absolutely nothing had happened. Except that I had massaged her little back and that with all clothes still on.

It took quite a while before I could speak to my eldest in private. She admitted the incest story. She said she had lied because she had been angry against daddy about something and then she had concocted that story. I asked her to repeat this confession also to her mother, but that she refused to do: "Is that absolutely necessary, Dad? It is so long ago!" With that the story should have ended but it didn't. During the 30-40 years that followed my number one daughter would repeat these accusations with regularity. To me, to her siblings, to my friends and to God knows whom else. Just as many times she would acknowledge that it was all not true. To my best (male) friend she once said: "Between Papa and me never anything happened that we should be ashamed of." I cannot make it any clearer. Which did not prevent her from a year later declaring to her sisters that this incest had ruined her life and that it had left her with a life-long trauma. Traces of Ma? More than just a few. This daughter continually tried to be the victim; the very same psychosis as with her mother and her maternal grandmother. Then it was this professor, then that teaching assistant, then her colleagues in Edmonton. She forever was finding reasons to be the victim.

One particular story kept crossing through her life and our family for years; the story of Paul. When she was 15-16 we had sent her to the Netherlands for six months in order to have a good taste of Dutch school and culture. Our friends Paul and Helen took her into their family, where they had two daughters of about the same age. A few days after having returned from that sojourn she confessed to me that she was pregnant of this Paul. Lotte and I of course were shocked; the first thing we did was taking her to our family physician. He discovered that she was not pregnant at all. When I took him aside for a minute, he added that there was absolutely no internal damage that he could discern. In the meantime I had already phoned Pal and in my anger I had told him what I thought of him now that our daughter had declared to be pregnant of him. His reaction was remarkable, if only because of his choice of words: "That is impossible, Gus. If she is pregnant it must be from somebody else".

OK, she was not pregnant but just as evidently something had happened. Was my oldest daughter lying? It took another 10-15 years before I could solve this riddle. I arranged a meeting with Paul, who in the meantime had sold his factory and who was quietly enjoying his retirement. He had done away with his heavy drinking and also his chasing of wild women. He admitted that in that time he had planned to 'make a woman' out of my daughter as well as of his own daughters. He maintained, however, that in the end nothing at all had come of that plan. Yes, the underpants had been off, but he 'had not had a sexual relation with her' to quote Bill Clinton. He admitted that there had been 'a Monica Lewinski situation' as it was called then. Paul showed himself utterly repentant; this event had in effect changed his whole life. His credibility was enhanced because of the small details he mentioned, which I had heard already from my daughter. 'Perpetrator knowledge' it is called in police jargon. He had prepared a glass of hot milk for her, to which he had added a heavy shot of vodka. He mentioned also the *fl.*25 banknote that he later had put on her night table. Daughter had found the banknote and she had put it happily into her purse. Payment for services rendered? Reward? Silencing money? Is my daughter the first prostitute in the family? Paul had completely convinced me; now my sweet daughter. At the first opportunity I put the question very directly to her: "Has Paul been with his penis into your vagina, yes or no?" "Ach Papa, that is so long ago, I can't remember that."

My daughter is therefore the only woman in the world who in full consciousness has been deflowered by a person well known to her and who cannot remember it. On the other hand the never-happened incest by her father (who, by the way, would only have touched her nipples), which supposedly had happened some five years earlier, she remembered daily. Yeah, yeah, fodder for psychologists; this daughter, for all her youth, was already a full-blown psychotic.

Even more remarkable is the attitude of ex-wife Lotte. She has done literally everything to destroy Gus. The weapon of a false incest accusation she could have used to perfection in this undertaking, but she never did this. Nothing is so effective and so destructive as a false accusation of abuse. It leaves the victim to prove his innocence. Professionals fear it, because it is devilishly difficult to obtain a clear-cut yes or no decision. Around me in my own professional world I have seen it happen. I have seen reputations and careers being destroyed by slanderous students. Now we have three known generations of psychotics in our family and soon there will be four as soon as the oldest child of our oldest daughter will reach puberty. All told, Lotte had delivered another enigma.

XXXIX

France

During that Sabbatical, Lotte had really conducted herself marvelously. I had obligations for a speakers tour in Japan, India, Pakistan and some more places in the Middle East, such as Iran and Iraq. Therefore I had left weeks earlier, making a round-the-world trip turning left, *i.e.* Westward. Lotte left home a few weeks later taking the East-bound route. After a number of weeks we re-united in Paris. Lotte had in the meantime transferred our home to a renter, had packed all the luggage and had flown to Paris with the children. There an apartment was awaiting her, but many other things had to be organized. The children ended up in three different schools. Next she presented herself to the *Préfecture* for a residence permit. There was a rental contract to be signed, food to be purchased and courses to be found for ourselves to improve our French.

The period in France was a kind of cease fire. We did all kinds of interesting things. Such as wander around all of Paris, exploring everything such as the *Marché des Puces* (the famous flea market) and attending Mass in the *Notre Dame,* which was only five minutes walking from our apartment. We visited the *Louvre* countless times, partly because entrance is free on Sundays. Naturally we visited friends and family in the Netherlands. I had quickly bought a Volvo station wagon which I had taken possession of right at the factory in Göteborg in Sweden. We made trips in the neighboring area, then a long weekend to see the castles of the Loire and finally a long camping trip through all of France. What to say about Lotte in this period? Only that her illness seemed to have receded to the background. She showed herself the good comrade, on whom I could always count to do the necessary. In the meantime she too seemed to enjoy all the adventures and all new experiences. However, no love, no trace of it, no affection; don't ever think that. Yes, sex, plenty of sex even; she insisted on that, but no love. The sabbatical ended in December and that in itself presented a special undertaking.

XL

Male Chauvinist Pig

We wanted to start implementing our agreement as soon as possible. An addition would be built to our home, an annex, being a complete suite with living room, bedroom plus bathroom. A live-in house keeper would be hired to do all the house work and to attend to the children whenever Lotte and I were engaged with the University. Before the winter was actually gone, a coal and straw fire was lit on the building site to thaw the frozen ground. It took about two weeks for the heat of this fire to eat its way through and then the digging could start. Half a year later the annex was finished so that we could start thinking about the next phase. Lotte was busy preparing a course in Computer Science she was going to give, again as sessional Instructor. This was a new course for her. Our agreement still stood but that did not mean that there was peace; quite to the contrary. Lotte felt betrayed by life and I was of course the culprit. In spite of that, a new element was creeping into our conversations. As I mentioned earlier Lotte was not entirely wrong. She was right on a different level compared to her chosen battle field. Lotte's situation was not unique. There were many sessional instructors on this Campus. The budget problems were real and the University saw these temporary teaching staff as an inexpensive way to continue offering the widest possible palette of courses. No social charges, no pension premiums, no health insurance and yet often very good quality of teaching. Our University was no different in this respect than any other in Canada. At a certain moment a full 30% of all courses was given by these contract teaching staff. One could say that the situation was unfair. Some went so far as to say that the University was guilty of slave labor.

There was another side to it, though. Economic down turn or not, the University was obliged to provide the best possible education with the budget available. Also, most of these Sessionals did not want it differently. The system was extremely flexible; you were hired by semester and you could always say "no", if you wanted to do something else for the moment. And say "yes" the next time. For most the extra income was not important; often the taxman took half of it and the remainder was often spent on extra babysitting, cleaning women and the like. In spite of all that many did it in order to be engaged in something intellectual. Indeed, most of them were wives of professors, with their husbands bringing in a good income. With that the prospect of women's discrimination entered the discussion. Everywhere in the country Faculty Associations were created, a sort of Labor Unions for professors. Soon also these sessional Instructors were admitted. People like Lotte who felt perhaps discriminated could turn to their Faculty Association for help. As a matter of fact our Faculty Association became really interested in the point of sessional Instructors and it began to exert pressure on the Administration.

Around this time I personally began to take an interest in the general point of discrimination. There were a fair number of people potentially affected, Lotte amongst them. Lotte wasn't even the one with the strongest arguments. Some of them gave even two courses each semester plus Summer courses, so that the whole amounted to a full time job. These were people, often single women with children who were the sole bread winner, who did this work for a living. All these people, with the exception of Lotte, asked the University for permanency of their jobs. In the end all of them, again with the exception of Lotte, launched a formal complaint against the University, supported in this by the Faculty Association. I followed from very close the cases of five of these Instructors. In the end all of them won their case. This was not easy, for nobody; the budget restraints were very real, but it did happen. The solutions were different in all cases. Creative solutions were found even though these were costly for the University. In the end, all these Sessional Instructors, who had often worked for many years for the University, and who had asked for a remedy, got their permanent appointment with pension, with all social benefits. A female colleague of Lotte in the Math Department got a permanent part-time appointment as Lecturer, a rank which had never existed at this University, but one that she insisted on. Another was sent away for a year, to obtain a PhD elsewhere, all paid for by the University. She indeed managed to do this and subsequently received an appointment as Assistant Professor with tenure. And so forth. They all got what they wanted, all except Lotte. But then, Lotte never formally applied.

If Lotte had shown a little bit of patience, if she too had submitted an official request, if she too had sought the help of the Faculty Association, then she too would have received what she wanted. Or, what she said she wanted. Now that the time had come when the Administration really went to work to solve the problems around the Sessionals, she lost all interest. Soon thereafter she gave up all her teaching work. Conclusion: Lotte did not want to see her problems solved, she wanted to complain and she wanted to feel unhappy. And above all she wanted to destroy me and in that she would not succeed when all her demands were granted. Destroying me that was her first priority; the rest was just camouflage. Not that I felt that way at that time, far from it. That hard conclusion I reached only years later, many years later, after our divorce had taken effect already years past. The conclusion that I did reach at the time was simply that Lotte did not want a professorate because she was scared silly that she might fail, never mind that she had been so successful as a Sessional Instructor.

I will never say that Lotte was a bad person. I have told of her many good qualities. Unfortunately Ma's kind of psychosis had also taken hold of Lotte. Now she felt slighted, betrayed by everything and everyone. Two statements of hers that I heard often illustrate this:

"The world (society) is a male conspiracy to keep all women down", and
"All men are chauvinist pigs, the only difference being that some are worse than others".

This again she always said in English even when she had a discussion with me in Dutch. When Lotte began to scold she used English.

Major societal changes always happen slowly. Every existing system had its reasons for coming into being, in this particular way. Otherwise it would never have become a societal system in the first place. When changes become desirable or necessary one cannot just throw out the old system. First the new parts have to be thought through very carefully. If you neglect this, as do the anarchists, then all kinds of injustices arise which are often worse than the perceived old problems. The sixties and seventies were such a breakpoint in our societal development with many changes, such as the women's emancipation.

Lotte was smart enough to know that the immediate granting of her wishes was an impossibility; that is exactly why she posed her complaints that way. She did not want a solution, she wanted to complain forever, because she wanted to permanently feel unhappy. That was the essence of Ma's psychosis, then Lotte's psychosis and a generation later that of our oldest daughter. In this sick reference frame it is logical to attack who is closest and what is nearest. That is why I was attacked, just like Ma had attacked her three eldest children, when Pa turned out to be an unassailable fortress.

In this atmosphere the *dénouement* came down like a rock although, admittedly, it had a logic of its own. The addition to our home was almost finished and we placed an advertisement in the local newspaper to find a house keeper. We had even a few interviews and then Lotte said, all of a sudden: "No, I am stopping with this. You have to become that house keeper". And with that short little sentence we were back at the starting point. I was to give up my research and would be allowed to go to the university only in the mornings. I would have to look after the children, do all the cleaning, make the beds and cook the meals. Why all that again? If Lotte wanted a career she could have it; it was not necessary to destroy mine. The children were growing up, now in the 10-16 year bracket so they were becoming more and more independent. Lotte would have plenty of time to develop herself. In fact she did so but without academic focus. What on earth might be her hidden agenda, apart from the apparent one of wanting to destroy me?

Did I not have even better reasons to feel betrayed? Betrayed by my own partner-for-life? This new development threw me literally for a loop. For the longest time I did not know what to do. If I gave in to her demands this would have grave consequences. Being fired from my position was a likelihood. If I did not give in I would forever been stuck with an angry, scolding and very unhappy spouse. In fact, I still loved her enough to absolutely not want that. With hindsight it sounds ridiculous but in fact I did consider for a long period to do what Lotte demanded and to accept that I would be fired. I knew enough about my own Department to know that they would not accept this houseman plan. I tried to find help, but where could I find such help that Lotte would go along with it? It had been for twenty years nothing but *nada, njet* and now again there was no change in her attitude. Lotte kept repeating her demands and kept maintaining that there was nothing wrong with our marriage. She saw nothing wrong with her demands and if I did, well, that was clearly my fault, not hers. Therefore no need for a psychologist; that was clearly only a trick to get her in the madhouse. "Listen Lotte, that would never work unless there is a clear medical reason for it. And if there is no such reason as you maintain what is there then to fear?" I had on my own initiative already spoken extensively with psychiatrists and psychotherapists and I was still walking around a free man?! Clearly, at this stage Lotte had lost contact with the real world. This smelled of schizophrenia; at the very least her fear for being locked up was psychopathic just like her persecution complex. Ma with her enforced stays in psychiatric wards was never far away. I was literally at the end of my powers and possibilities. However, it would still get worse. Suddenly Lotte decided that she would accept outside help. And that became the beginning of the end. The problem at hand was already too taxing for me. I had no inkling that it could get much worse. It could and it did.

XLI

The Opus Dei Weekend

Anyone remembering the movie: "The Eiger Sanction"? A rental murderer has a contract to eliminate another murderer. Almost all he has to go on to identify his victim is that he is a mountain climber and that he has a problem with one of his legs so that he sometimes limps. Finally he finds his man during a climbing excursion of the Eiger mountain. Then there is an accident, a fall; his victim is hanging on a single rope. All he has to do is to let the safety rope slip.

I ended up in a situation that I later called the Red River Sanction. All of a sudden Lotte came with a proposal. She wanted to attend with me a Marriage Encounter weekend. A (female) colleague of hers from the Math Department had participated and had come back with highly positive tales. Originally this was organized by the *Opus Dei* movement in Europe, but it had spread worldwide and it was now also active outside the Roman Catholic Church as a non-denominational organization. In our case the weekend was given in a former monastery of the Oblate Fathers but, apart from a single priest, the weekend was led by lay volunteers.

We started by driving to the monastery on a Friday evening and we heard how the weekend was organized. The next morning we got home work! We were to write a love letter to our partner. The idea was then to exchange these letters and to discuss these with each other, if desired with the help of one of the leaders. Possibly certain experiences could be shared in the entire group. We departed to our rooms. Our room had a small ante-chamber and that is where I sat myself down to write my letter while Lotte went to the larger bedroom.

I had no trouble to write my love letter. I wrote that I still loved her very much that she and only she was my princess, with whom I desired to spend the remainder of my living days. I added that I would do anything within my powers to make her happy. Honestly, I put all that into that letter, all my feelings and also my hope that we would succeed in improving our relation. Contentedly I went to Lotte and gave her my letter.

"Here is my letter".

"Thank you".

She read my letter in silence, then folded it and put it into her purse. I had been watching her face intently, hoping for a sign of emotion; none appeared.

"How about your letter", I asked.

"I don't have a letter and there won't be any".

She said it very quietly, almost businesslike. My love letter I have never seen again; neither did she ever refer to it at a later time. Why then would she nevertheless want it?

Did you ever hear the expression: "My stomach became as hard as a football"? I can now state that such a description is very apt. That was precisely what I felt when Lotte delivered this latest blow to me. My stomach became hard and felt as large as a football. Then I felt it shrinking and getting harder until I had a stone in my stomach the size of an orange. My memory of this moment is so vivid that I can still feel it again. For twenty years I had still hoped to win Lotte's heart. At every turn she had let me slide a little bit further down; now the rope was entirely loose and I fell in a free fall. Now she had said "no" to my love for her in a complete and definitive way. She had said it without compassion, without feeling, without any sign of emotion, at least as far as I could see. She had kicked me in the underbelly and she had done it as hard as she could. How on earth did she manage to do such a thing?

At that moment the priest knocked at our door. He was making the rounds to see how far we were. Briefly I informed him what had transpired and he then spoke to Lotte:

"It does not have to be a real love letter. Perhaps you could write a letter to your husband saying that you too would want to work on the problems in your marriage?"

"No way. I don't want to write any letter, most certainly not a nice letter to him".

"Then perhaps a friendship letter?"

"This man is no friend", Lotte cut him off.

Shaking his head, the priest left, most likely wondering what had moved this woman to come to this 'Encounter'. Of course that is what I wondered myself. Lotte had apparently listened to the story of her colleague and had responded, without realizing that undoubtedly she would be asked to provide a positive contribution herself. Strange; did she really believe that something good would come out if it if we both would not put something into it ourselves? Mere naivety? With a shock I realized that perhaps from her deepest subconsciousness she might have done this deliberately, just to force the issue. Had she realized, however, that she would be asked to say that she loved me or that she considered me her friend or any such nice thing about me, then she would never have proposed it. Of that I am sure. The proof is the ice-cold, unbending, uncompromising rejection that she subsequently displayed.

The furniture in this retreat home perhaps at one time had been meant for young men aspiring to become priests. It was lacking all comfort. For me this was pure torture. My back problem, always latently present, showed up. The extra stress of the moment required that I needed more comfort, not less. I could not find a single chair that could give me some relief. The real pain was located somewhere else, I realized that full well. What should I do? What could I do? I really saw no way out anymore and no hope for any improvement. Hadn't I tried already everything possible at least ten times? All I could do now was wait and hope the situation would clear by itself. I was not thinking divorce, absolutely not. All my attempts had been focused on finding solutions. How could I make Lotte happy?

Downstairs in the lobby there was a table with all kinds of books and other materials that were for sale. In the back row I saw a Jerusalem Bible. I had heard about it. That Bible had been written jointly by Catholic, Protestant and Jewish Bible experts, translated from the oldest, most original texts. I reached forward (doubtless with stretched knees) in order to pick up that Bible, but that did not work. On that moment lightning shot through my body. When I came to, I found myself on the ground squirming in terrible pain. Something had happened in my back; the slightest movement caused pain shoots, that made me shout in agony. It was Sunday afternoon; one more chapel meeting and the Encounter would be over. A nun offered to stay with me. She admitted that she had some valium tablets; would I like some? Yes, that was a bright idea and gratefully I took two tablets. After the chapel meeting was over, another young woman came over to me. She said that she was a nurse and that she knew exactly what was wrong with me. According to her it was a vertebrae disc that pressed against the spinal cord. She also knew how to reduce the pain. Gently she pulled at both my legs, while somebody else held tight to my arms. What a relief! Unfortunately she could not maintain that position in eternity and when she released my legs I cried out in pain again. In the meantime an ambulance had been ordered and shortly after that I was on my way to the hospital. There I saw Lotte for the first time since it started. She had a Jerusalem Bible in her hand. She said that I had asked her to buy that Bible and that was what she had done. I did not remember any of that but it may well have been the truth. I still have that Bible; my beautiful love letter I have never seen again.

So began a new phase in my life, that of a sick, handicapped person. With hindsight it is not too difficult to understand what had happened and why it had happened at this particular moment. Stress, enormous amounts of stress had built up in my body. My scientific work was also often very stressful, but results and victories had also been part of it, so that I could live with it. The continuing marriage problems without solutions caused stress that was even more intensive. Then came the high expectations of the Marriage Encounter; also causing stress, but of the better kind. And then the disaster! The psychosomatic system then searches for the weakest spot in the body in order to strike exactly there. Without hesitation the lower back was singled out as the most vulnerable spot and there the attack was directed at. And so I was felled. Perhaps not a very big deal. Such hernia's happen very often with tall men in the 40+ group. Usually the patient walks again after three months and after six months he may be at work again.

I had no idea, however, that my illness would last more than ten years, that in fact I would never work anymore (apart from two short trial periods) and that this would eventually lead to a divorce.

I was barely fifty years old, at the top of my career. I also had three young children. Oh yes, and a wife too.

XLII

Sick and Ill

April is a good time to fall ill. I had only a few more lectures to give and those were taken over by my colleagues. Then there were still the final exams for two classes. I went back to exams I had given in earlier years because I felt not able to construct new exam questions. The severity of my problem became evident when these written exam booklets came back to me; I had to read and to grade them. I had extreme problems just to concentrate on the written material and to evaluate it. In my profession this ought to be rather routine but this time I did not succeed in grading these papers within the required ten days. When I failed to hand in the exams and their grades in time, the Head was not pleased.

In the end I spent the remainder of that Spring plus the entire Summer in the so-called recreation room of our home. This room was half under and half above zero-level, a sort of basement but then with large windows and sufficient sunlight as a consequence. There I tried to get better, mostly just lying on my bed. It wasn't easy. I still had much pain, particularly at night when I moved my limbs during my sleep. Often I would wake up from my own cries of pain. The bathroom was close by; if I could just crawl till I could get to the shower then I cold quieten these shoots of pain. I would pull myself up by the shower pipes and then the hot water could massage the muscles. Pain killers and sometimes a sleeping pill also helped. Even the entire medical profession could do no more for me. By resting, that disc had to go back to its original position and then no longer press against the spinal nerve. Later in the Summer I learned to walk again and I could even reach the spousal bed three levels higher. By September I could walk almost normally. And so I began to prepare myself for the return to my professoral duties. I had lost a costly Summer for my scientific research. So far my illness had shown an almost standard pattern. So many other men of middle age with a sedentary kind of work situation had experienced a similar problem only to get back into the saddle after six months or so.

My return to teaching was not so easy, though. I could barely sit upright, so I walked up and down a lot. Standing still was painful and that was something I often had to do while writing things on the black board. I then began to use an overhead projector, which required me to sit down. To counteract the sit-down problems I rolled my best desk chair from my room to the class room. It must have been quite a sight to see this professor going through the corridors while pushing his wheeled desk chair which carried an overhead projector. Sometimes the pain became so excruciating that I had to push my back with all force against a wall. Often the sweat was running down my face while I fought desperately to finish the hour. I also tried to get my research going again.

I had received a large grant which had enabled me to purchase the most modern equipment and I was determined to work with that equipment in an optimum way. Such machines remain modern only a very short time and then there are again new developments. Soon you might be left with 'old-fashioned' equipment that was only a few years old.

I managed to remain active the entire Fall semester; in fact I also got through the next Winter semester. Fortunately I had only a light teaching load; however, leading my research group was very taxing. Somehow I had to keep my people busy in a useful manner. That meant giving advice, planning the next moves, but also ordering supplies and keeping the equipment in running shape. I also had to run to the Library to read the newest papers and to find needed information. In addition I wanted to speak with colleagues in the land, prepare guest lectures, attend conferences and symposia. And then, finally the most difficult task of all: to write papers for scientific journals. I had a number of Masters and PhD students and also a postdoctoral Fellow. Incredibly, I got my research and the papers going again, but the price was high. In my office there was a poster showing a grinning fellow hanging lazily in his chair. The undertitle read: *"Sometimes I do nutting; I just sits here"*. Indeed for the uninitiated passer-by it might appear that I was doing nothing; in fact I was charging up my batteries. The pain was constantly there, the whole day. Constantly I was pushing myself across that pain barrier, just to continue working. The body reacts then by getting tired and by demanding rest.

At home the situation was perhaps marginally better; at least there were comfortable chairs, specially selected by me way back for the back support they provided. In bed I was OK as long as I stayed flat on my back. Whenever I (or Lotte) moved, the back would react again, sometimes with agonizing shoots of pain. My conjugal obligations (and pleasures) suffered under these conditions and here again a little tragedy would develop. Lotte had always allowed only one position, the so-called missionary position. With this position I had to bend my back just the wrong way. This hollow bending was always hurting; making love while fighting an acute pain is not exactly satisfactory, let alone enjoyable. Therefore I asked Lotte for a different position, with Lotte on top. She understood the reason for my request and therefore she tried it. However, this is not just a mechanical variant; it is the upper person who has to take the initiative and that was too much for Lotte. "This I cannot do", she said after a few seconds and she slid off me. Never, never could she even pretend a little affection for me. I might misunderstand that she was caring a bit for me! Therefore better no sex and that was a great sacrifice for her.

In this phase Lotte showed no interest in my illness. After all, the medical people had said that I needed rest and that then all would turn out OK. However, that did not happen. In fact the situation got worse as time went on. I felt that I could not bear it much longer. Either I had to call in sick again or I had to think up something else. I did the latter by asking for another sabbatical. True enough, I had not worked the required six years for it but I told the Dean that my body needed this resting period. The Dean agreed; he too realized that I could not go much longer anyhow. This time I decided to stay in Canada. The choice fell on Montreal where, at the *Université de Montréal,* I was welcomed. Number one daughter did Anthropology at the same University and the other two went to *Collège St. Jean Bréboeuf* and *Collège Marie de France,* respectively. Two famous schools of the French system for the perpetuation of the French language as a superior world language. Lotte was busy setting up the housekeeping in a new environment but very quickly she became the nurse for a handicapped husband. I was treated well by my colleague and his research group and I was provided with everything I needed. I was asked to speak English only! There, in Québec, another emancipation struggle had taken place to recognize the Francophone roots of the Québec people. That struggle they had taken very far; there existed a real language police. All advertising, billboards, restaurant menus had to be in French and French only. Those poor students of the *Université de Montréal* barely had the opportunity to hear English and to practice speaking it. For someone who is seeking a career in the world of Science this is almost deadly.

I held out for no more than two or three weeks. The day that would end in such cruel finality began so nicely. The sky was blue, almost a Mediterranean deep blue. A soft gentle sun warmed everything and everyone. The first brown leaves whispered under your feet. I had a parking permit for the entire Campus but you still had to find an empty spot. I found one on a high outcrop, close to my destination, a room in the Chemistry building. In order to avoid a lengthy detour I let myself slide down that grassy knoll. Now to the door and the elevator. It was costing all too much effort and lots of sweat. Puffing and gasping and in considerable back pain I managed to reach my room, sat myself down into a chair and waited until the pain would subside. After an hour and a half I still sat there, panting and the pain was still there in full force. I knew that I had to give up the unequal fight. With slow gestures I collected my research papers, got up, locked my room and found my way back to the parking lot. Slowly I drove home and told Lotte that I could not continue. It was clear that I had to stay home until the situation would improve.

XVIII

Handicapped

Via friends I sought and found medical help. Montreal had very good hospitals, in part founded by Scottish surgeons. I ended up in a rather small hospital of the British tradition of three centuries. The orthopedic surgeon where I ended up with was also rather small, but with her 155 cm she radiated much authority. With her somewhat brisk manners she made me feel in good hands with her. She immediately said that she was not of a mind to operate on me, this under loud protestations of her assistant who was doing a stage with her. He had hoped for a nice disc removal, but his boss would have nothing of it. Much rest, muscle relaxants and pain killers, that was it. A month later there was absolutely no improvement, though. The little lady then proposed an epidural injection of cortisone. As it happened, this hospital had a specialist on staff, who apparently was very good with it. This doctor told me he had performed hundreds of these injections into the spine and he wanted to inject me too. He pushed and pushed, replaced the needle by a thicker one when the first one bent, until I finally blacked out. When I woke up, a lovely Philippine nurse was holding my hand. That was nice as it was, of course, but I had lost interest in further attempts by the doctor-with-the-needle. I shuddered to think what might happen if in the end his needle would indeed penetrate and then would end up penetrating my spinal cord.

Next stop was the acupuncture doctor. This man was indeed a medical doctor, graduated from the famous McGill University in Montreal, who had specialized in acupuncture, as witnessed by the many framed-in diplomas from China and France which were decorating the walls of his waiting room. He began with putting very fine needles everywhere in my body: in my ear lobes, my ear flaps, nose, brows, cheeks, chest, arms, toes and fingers. Connected to these needles were wires which led to a piece of equipment that could put electrical current on these wires. Putting in the needles did not hurt at all; when he next put a current through these needles I began to feel a tickling sensation. Next he put the needles closer to the pain spots in my back. The pain was still bearable, although the treatment made me groan. Finally he found the sorest spot, right next to the disc that was causing all the trouble. Again he turned on the current; I let go of a primal scream and then lost consciousness. After a while I came to. I heard the doctor speaking to me: "Wake up, sir, wake up", but I could not reply. The doctor then walked away into another room; apparently he was treating several patients at the same time. Once and a while he came back to see how I was doing. At a certain moment I was ready to live again and I sat straight up, with my legs hanging over the bedside. "Good, good", he beamed, "you very great pain, you doing good. Now stand up. You can do." And indeed, I could stand up and I walked a few steps. Miracle! I felt no pain! I could even walk to the car that was parked a block away. I hadn't walked that far in months. Splendid. However, there were disadvantages too with this acupuncture treatment. To begin with, the effect was only temporary. The doctor said I needed three treatments a week. I negotiated that down to twice a week. That was important because each treatment was costing me $50.00 cash; the insurance did not pay a cent for this alternative medicine. And the doctor did not believe in giving receipts! I was living on 80% of my salary with extremely high school costs for my children and I simply could not afford the good doctor for very long. Then, every time there was this awful pain, just before blacking out again. That in itself was traumatic. It made me think of the Nazis and their torture techniques. In spite of that, every time again I pulled myself up, submitting to this voluntary torture session.

In all of this Lotte was again a super care giver. She drove me wherever I needed to go and she was certainly also thinking ahead. She insisted, for example, that I should buy a walking cane. I was against that, because who wants to show off his physical problem? In reality that cane was a solution to several problems. We found one that could be adjusted in length. It also had a very wide grip; it had been designed for people with rheumatic hands. I found a different application though. As soon as we were halting for a moment, then I would sit down on that cane. The wide hand grip became a mini-seat. Of course the cane emphasized that I had a problem. In a short while I had become a crippled bent-over little old man who shuffled slowly forward. Lotte did more. On a certain day she came back from a garage sale where she had found a bean bag. That is a large pillow made of plastic or leather, filled for three quarters with little pieces of plastic foam. From that day onward that bean bag was my constant companion. It was impossible to destroy the thing. I threw it down somewhere and then I let myself fall into it. The bag formed itself around the shape of my body and that gave me maximum support. Then Lotte saw something in a furniture store. It was a kind of easy chair with leather cushions in a steel frame. The whole thing was mounted on a large steel ring and it could therefore rotate and turn in any direction; a knob then could be used to tighten and fix the chosen position. The back support could be adjusted for any angle; very novel was then that the seat would move forward and upward to give maximum comfort. Another knob could adjust the support in the lower back region. Lotte had dragged me almost to this shop so that I could try out the thing. She also pointed out that there was a special price tag hanging from it; priced down from $1500.00 to $1199.00. Still an enormous price for a chair but she was right; this was exactly what I needed. We bought it and from that moment onward I practically lived in that chair. Again this was the good side of Lotte, she was caring in a manner that a professional nurse could not have bettered. In the condition where I found myself I did not reflect on what she did not have.

The remainder of that sabbatical year I stayed at home. What did I do with my time? Watching TV, for example; I discovered soon that I had an ever increasing problem here. I had the greatest of difficulty trying to keep track of the story line and to remember the personages. The same with reading the newspaper or a book. I indeed read a few books but I remember nothing of it. Years later, watching a movie on TV, I recognized a certain scene, but only that scene and nothing else. It was evident that I had seen that movie before but that very little of it had been stored in my brains. I had made great plans regarding participating in the cultural life of Montreal but nothing came of it. In spite of it all I wanted very much to see an opera. Lotte began to investigate the possibilities. And those existed indeed. With the aid of a volunteers organization I was delivered at a personnel entrance of the opera building and from there it went per wheelchair through all kinds of corridors to my reserved seat. Afterwards Lotte was awaiting me at the same side entrance. I remember all those details very sharply but which opera did play? Nothing of the opera itself was stored. I remember only that I did enjoy it tremendously. I had another source of diversion. Without having any concrete plan in mind I had taken my stamp collection of Curaçao along on my sabbatical tour. Also I took along a book on the postal history of those Antillean islands. That book had just been published and now I tried to do something with it. That was hard. Many passages in the book I had to read repeatedly in order to really grasp the contents, store it and recall it when needed. The collection was set up all afresh on blank pages, purely chronologically with handwritten notes on dates, design, numbers, printing technique and so on. In order to be able to do this work I knelt down on the floor, using a coffee table as my working desk. This job progressed only very slowly; on the average I produced one page a day. Then body and mind were exhausted. Holding up in this fashion was due in great part to the little doctor, who had me equipped with a steel corselette. The steel ribs were packaged in leather, but steel is steel so that my back received a solid support. Small leather straps served to tighten the unit; sometimes I felt like a 18th century woman with her wasp waist. In this way only I could stand or sit or kneel for a little while. It was really not much for an intellectual like me; when the album was finished shortly before we left Montreal for home I was as proud as a peacock.

We had good friends in Montreal, a couple of which the female half had been a senior nurse and who had had several executive administrative functions in the world of hospitals. She visited me quite a number of times but she too did not find the key to my ailing. She told me that evidently I was ill, very ill even. She saw that in the feverish way of my speaking and acting. She also saw that I was in great pain, but she could not discover where the problem really was located. She was of the opinion that the spinal disc was not the only problem, but further than that she could not go. She was not the only one in that; the little doctor did not know it either and said that she did not know what to suggest. I decided to ask second opinions. Yet another orthopedic surgeon, again more bending, turning, twisting and so on. He too declared not to know what really ailed me and why I did not get better after rest. He gave me the advice to prepare myself that I would not get better ever; according to him there was nothing that the medical world could do for me anymore. That was a bitter pill to swallow! Not getting better ever. I wrote a sorrowful letter to the Head of my Department, warning him of the advice I had just received. And that he better start looking for a permanent replacement for me. There was one little ray of hope still. The little doctor had given me a referral to a famous surgeon in Toronto. I had to wait six months but finally the day was there. Once more I found a surgeon of the proud Scottish tradition. I have forgotten his name, so I will call him Old Mac. He tested me for a few minutes and then declared that he could do nothing for me. Again! However, he added that he did not understand why I had been referred to him. I told him a few things, who I was and how I had ended up in this predicament. He then loosened up a bit. He showed me what kind of surgeon he was. In fact he was just preparing some slides for a presentation at an international Conference. He showed me pictures of terribly contorted spines. He explained how he with rods, bolts and nuts succeeded in straightening these backs. He continued: "You don't need any of this, but you have three problems. To begin with there is that disc but that one is no worse that many others. In principle you still have your basic mobility; the conservative treatment that has been prescribed for you is the correct one. For God's sake, however, throw away that harness. That will make a complete cripple of you if you continue wearing it. Secondly you have a very serious pain problem. Find a specialized pain clinic, even if you have to travel far for it, That pain is your largest enemy, your most serious problem. Finally, you are severely depressed. Make sure you get treated for it; what you need is a good psychologist, not a psychiatrist, though."

I showed my surprise upon hearing the latter because he was the first of a long list of medical and paramedical professionals, who had looked at me and who had never even given a hint in that direction. Old Mac held to it saying that practically all his patients were seriously depressed, so he surely had some experience. "I noticed it already when you came shuffling in. I bet you were not shuffling in that manner after these acupuncture treatments". That was true; I had indeed noticed myself how I was deftly stepping after such a treatment. I told Old Mac that I had thought of depression myself, particularly because my problems were not going away, but that the various medical people had laughed that option away.

Old Mac promised that he would put his thoughts on paper for my doctors in Montreal. He did so indeed, but through a postal strike in Montreal this report arrived only months later on the desk of my little doctor. Fortunately, I could almost *verbatim* repeat to her what the Great Wise Man in Toronto had told me. She showed her great surprise regarding his diagnosis of severe depression. "I have seen indeed nothing of that, but perhaps you are an example of the 'smiling depressive', of which I have heard but which I have never encountered before."

I could kick myself. There I had been working so hard to accept my fate and the result had been that I had misled dozens of medical professionals. All, except Old Mac. I do still have that report by Old Mac; each time I read it I am hit by the absurdity of the situation. How particularly highly intelligent, perceptive, sensitive people, including those in medical professions, including also myself, are capable of fooling themselves and their environment. By sheer intellectuality they force themselves to accept matters that they never ought to have accepted. Most certainly not when something or someone is radiating warning signals.

There was nothing further that could be done until we got home again. That in itself presented a problem. How was I, in my condition, to get home, some 4,000 km away? By airplane and wheel chair, and then Lotte having to drive home by herself and the children? Air travel was fast but that promised to be a very uncomfortable journey. On the other hand, the trip to Toronto had taught me that Volvo seats with their many adjustment possibilities were made for people with back problems. So I decided to gamble and drive myself the distance. I begged Lotte for only one concession, that I would be allowed to drive on like a truck driver, because I did not think I could last more than three days. That was agreed and the trip went without a hitch, considerably helped by the bean bag, which at every stop was thrown against a tree with me in it.

XLIV

Calgary and Prozac

"One of your questions I can answer in five minutes", said Esther, "although this is not my habit. I prefer that my patients find the answers themselves, while I am assisting by opening doors, where they had not even suspected the presence of a door. So it will be with your second question, of why you are divorced. However, your first question of why you have been ill for so long is straight from the text books. Every self-respecting psycho therapist or psychologist ought to have known that, because it is really to be found in all kinds of books. As for myself I have encountered such a case before in my own practice, so I recognized it instantly, even while you were still telling your story. You fell ill and in particular you stayed ill, because this was the only way to save your marriage. Your ex-wife could not live with a normally functioning husband Gus. However, she also did not want to take the initiative to a divorce. She was afraid to live in poverty, quite apart from the moral burden in the eyes of family and friends. Therefore she did everything in her power to get you to start the divorce procedure. Formally the initiative had to come from you. Hence the scolding and the accusations of infidelity. The threats with the knife indicate that she was getting desperate, because it was quite risky what she was doing. What if you had gone to your family doctor with a request to have her locked up in a psychiatric ward of a hospital? Probably this would have worked, but you did not want that, Gus, because you loved her too much. She knew that and speculated that you would not do that. Your illness is therefore psychosomatic, Gus. Your spirit sought a weak spot and it found one in your body; that was not difficult. The pain is real, Gus, not imagined. That is how strong our spirit can be. With you as a handicapped person, your wife could play the dominant position. To the outside world she could show how she cared for you. Tell me, how good or how bad was your marriage during the illness?"

I was flabbergasted and angry at the same time. Why had no-one else noticed this before? Apparently I had been ill for some ten years and entirely needlessly so. Ten years of my life without any benefit and which I barely could remember. It was true that my pains were real. That had been measured at several occasions. By the Chinese doctor with his acupuncture but also later with electrodes that were placed in my neck and on my head. And indeed my marriage had never been so good as during my period of illness. During a rare moment of clarity I had remarked to Lotte: "Now that I am so sick, our marriage is much better, don't you agree?" Lotte had not replied; she had smiled her Mona Lisa enigmatic smile.

If only I had met Esther ten years earlier! All in all it was a miracle that I did meet her at all. I had gotten divorced, then I had left for the Netherlands for a period of six months in an attempt to find some rest. And then I had come home in an empty place. Lotte was staying with number one daughter refusing to come home. I should have made clever use of that fact but I didn't. I decided to leave the home and to move to another town about a day's travel away. I hoped that the distance would be sufficient to keep Lotte away from me. Naturally I had to change psychiatrist; I had become depressed again and so I was on Lithium and Prozac again. The new psychiatrist recommended to me was a friend of the previous one but he was very different. Already during my first visit I had asked him if he perhaps knew someone, a psychotherapist or a psychologist who might help me with a few questions. I had two conditions: it had to be a woman and she had to be at least as smart as I. Somewhere I still was harboring some hope. I foresaw, that at a certain time I would have to render account and then it would not do if a came up with a male chauvinist pig and certainly not with a weakling whom I could and would have manipulated. Robert, as was his name, began to laugh aloud and he said: "As chance will have it there is one such lady here in town who fits your conditions. Esther is a very smart lady and she is therefore in constant demand. I will try and see if she will see you". And so the memorable day came to be, when Esther and I met for the first time.

Robert did even more for me. At a certain moment I told him that low blood pressure was a genetic trait in me and that I therefore thought that the Lithium supplement was not useful or needed for me. Slowly the Lithium dose was diminished and then it became clear that a low Lithium content was normal for me. The 'natural' Lithium content in a person is determined by the environment and by the individual person. The range of 'normal' Lithium is extremely wide; I was on the low side but still within this range. Therefore Robert took a brave decision and took me off Lithium entirely. Since then I have never experienced even the slightest manic impulses, so why then had I swallowed Lithium for twelve years?

For the first time in years I began to feel a little better. It was over and I began to look at a life in the future. Hence the thought that perhaps I didn't need Prozac anymore either. I brought this up with Robert and he scratched his head: "Yeah, that is perhaps a possibility. After all, you are a type II depressive. You see, type I manic depressive people can go from a high into a deep down within a few days and then Prozac is too slow to remedy that. Just like all anti-depressiva Prozac needs three to six weeks to reach its full effectiveness. Type II persons on the other hand go much slower from top to bottom That usually takes hem three weeks or more and then there is enough time to take action with anti-depressiva." Hurrah, I was type II; at earlier occasions I had noticed that I reacted very fast on Prozac. Already after ten days I began to feel the effect. Therefore there was little risk and Robert let me slowly get off Prozac. Nothing happened; not then and not in the ten years thereafter. Why had my first psychiatrist this not done years ago? That answer I also found. I heard from Robert that his colleague had already had three court cases against him, each time when a patient of his died by suicide. The angry family charged him then with medical negligence or worse. True enough all three times he had been completely exonerated, both by Justice and by the Medical Disciplinary Chamber, but it had made him extremely careful; even with me he had not been willing to take any risk.

XLV

Catatonic

How to describe the next period, after that Montreal sabbatical year? It had not been a sabbatical at all. Rather than getting the batteries charged up again I had come home, sick and exhausted. I felt also very depressed. Defeated is perhaps the better word. I hardly existed any more. There was little left of my life and even less of my dreams. The psychiatrist put me on anti-depressiva again. At that time these were the so-called tricyclic compounds. Perhaps they did indeed work to keep my depression under control, but they had terrible side-effects. For example, I found it increasingly difficult to concentrate; reading or simply watching TV became empty activities. Later I learned the word 'catatonic'. In its extreme form not only the spirit but also the body becomes rigid. Arms, legs, fingers stick out stiffly, the mouth pulls open and makes only unintelligible sounds. With me it did not get quite that bad but it came close. It was as if my spirituality dried up entirely. Music, for example, I could not stand any more. All I heard was a cacophony of sounds which had no mutual connection. The radio was switched off for years. No gramophone record was played any more, and no radio program was listened to. Speaking was equally difficult. I could talk to only one person at the time and only for about fifteen minutes. After that it became too tiresome and I had to stop. In the early days colleagues would come by, but after a year or so they all stayed away. I simply did not exist anymore. What did I do with my time? Mostly nothing. Just sitting in my easy chair, sleeping a lot and, yes, watching TV if there was some sports program. Walking was very difficult. Sometimes I joined Lotte to a shopping mall. Then I was plunked down somewhere in a chair or on a bench, waiting until Lotte would pick me up again. That amounted to a tremendous performance. I did have a parking permit for handicapped, but even so I had stumbled from the entrance to that nearest bench. That might be as much as 20 m! Oh yes, I played with my stamps. Over the years that entire collection was rebuilt from a standard pre-printed album towards a set of heavy binders with blank pages organized according to my own views and ideas. Texts were added, written with drawing pens and East Indian black ink.

Slowly, very slowly, some progress was made. Imperceptibly almost unless you looked over the long run. Usually around Christmas, I made a sort of self-analysis. At that worst moment in Montreal I could walk only five steps. After a year that had expanded to ten steps. No one noticed; I was as handicapped as before.

Was there really nobody who could help? Was there nobody who could tell me what was ailing me? Well, the Great Wise Man had told me to find a pain clinic but there was none, not within 1000 km. That was something novel at the time and it had not penetrated yet into the interior. And that psychologist that I should have consulted? My family doctor had shaken his head when he heard that. In our town, really a city, there was not one psychologist or psycho therapist that he could recommend. In hindsight you could say that I had bad luck. In the end I had to move to a city some 1000 km away before I found one but that was ten years later. My psychiatrist kept repeating that he was not a psychologist and that he did not even want to be one. In fact he did not have the time for it. In this way years went by. There was a steady improvement in ability to walk, but that was purely mechanistic; my head, my spirit remained as sick as before. There was no discussion even that I could take up my work again. The insurance prolonged their payments on the basis of an annual report from the psychiatrist. After a few years he told me that he wanted to recommend an infinite term, saying in effect that I never would be able to return to work: "Even if you now would get rid of that chronic pain, you would not be able to catch up the lost time. Your entire body is weakened and so is your thinking power. The insurance Company knows that too. Someone who has been five years away from this very difficult work as a professor will never come back".

XLVI

Fighting Pain

And then a real miracle of sorts occurred. I heard a rumor about a new pain-fighting method. Well, it was a bit more than a rumor. Once a week a medical person came to our town who had elsewhere founded a pain clinic. Naturally I made an appointment with this doctor in one of our hospitals. I was treated with an instrument that sent electrical currents through the skin into my body. The theory was that the electricity would stimulate the brain into sending endorphins to the spot where the tingling originated. These endorphins are natural painkillers and so the body itself would fight the pain. Primitive as the method may sound, it did work. It would not work against the strong jolts of pain but it did reduce the chronic low-level pain. Was that worthwhile? I compare chronic pain with the Chinese water drop torture. One drop does not hurt, neither will ten drops. However, let these drops fall day and night on a person's forehead and the receiving person will become a jabbering idiot filled with pain. Chronic back pain is much the same; it never ceases and it eats constantly into your human integrity. This particular instrument was very primitive; I had to go to the hospital each time.

The instrument was tied around my middle, with the generator for tickling the nerves taped to my lower back and then I had to lay down for an hour or so. Then came the news that a much improved version was coming; the electrical stimulation would take place right inside the body. There was already a surgeon on hand in our town who had received the necessary training in the USA; after a discussion with this man I became the first person to receive a built-in pain fighter. The first in our town and one of the very first in Canada. Was I ever lucky to live in this rather isolated city and yet receive this novel surgery. In the Netherlands this same method was introduced only thirty years later! I was allowed to follow the operation live on a TV screen; there was only local anesthesia. This was essential because at a certain stage I had to help and tell the surgeon what I was feeling. A vertebra was drilled through with an electrical 3/8" drill bit to just before it would hit the central nerve. Next a pod with several small electrodes was placed into the hole, the electrodes touching the nerve. A second operation installed a radio receiver into my side with wires that were pulled through my body to connect with these electrodes. The surgeon manipulated the wires and the electrodes by moving them around and putting electrical current through them. Now came my turn in telling him when I felt a tingling and how strong this sensation was. After the best two positions were selected everything was closed up. On the outside I had a radio transmitter which was powered by a 9 volt battery and which was taped right opposite the buried receiver. The power unit was held on my belt. Then I switched the unit ON and a heavenly tingling filled my body. Soon enough I learned that an hour of switched-on was enough to chase the low-level pain away. As time went by, I needed this instrument less and less. After a couple of years I found that I could leave the instrument switched off for several days and after ten years I did not use it at all anymore. My body, or rather my brain, had learned to make these endorphins and send them to the pain spot when needed. Presently these electrodes and the radio receiver still sit inside my body. The only trouble they cause is with airport security devices.

XLVII

Adultery

Shortly after the implant of the electronic pain fighter my transition to Prozac took place. Freed of much of the chronic pain, Prozac did the rest. In very short order I became a normally functioning man again. This to great displeasure of Lotte who reacted on these developments with anger. To prove to her that I was a normal person again I made a three-week tour through the Netherlands, all by myself in a rented car, without in fact making even a single navigation error. Upon my return home Lotte had once more exploded. This was the start of a period which lasted about three years. While I worked on my condition, gaining in strength and beginning to live again, Lotte began to launch accusations of infidelity. Every week she presented new lover girls; in the end it became a harem of 32 women whom she mentioned by name and with whom I would have had a sex affair. "And these are only the ones of whom I am certain. I have the evidence! Plus those women I am suspecting. And then of course those women I happen to know nothing about as of to-day!"

The women she mentioned were all known individuals, friends from the University world. According to

Lotte I would have slept with practically all the wives of my colleagues in the Chemistry and Physics departments, truly a remarkable feat if it had been true. Initially I just waved these accusations away: "Stop this nonsense, Lotte. I have never even touched these women. This is ridiculous". Next I challenged her to come forward with that evidence she claimed to have. She came with a truly absurd piece of evidence. She had gone into the crawl space underneath our French church and there she had found a condom. This she now showed to me. The condom clearly had been used; lots of sand was still sticking to it. Triumphantly she showed me the thing which she held under my nose with a clothes peg. "I always wondered WHERE you did it, but here is the evidence". For Lotte this was proof absolute of my infidelity, although there was nothing that connected me to this used condom. In that time we did not even think of DNA analysis, but why would I have to prove my innocence? The point is that Lotte here had again left the real world. I do think that Lotte at those moments really believed in that fabricated truth. Later I discovered that Lotte at the same time also lived on a different level, the level of the real world. That point was made clear during the divorce proceedings. Here Lotte never claimed infidelity on my part as reason for the divorce, which is a standard thing to do in such circumstance. However, now she firmly believed in what she said; in this period she was psychotic and perhaps schizophrenic; yet on that other plane she also saw the real truth, meaning that these accusations were of a criminal nature. At the moment I was not really cognizant of that. I kept thinking: "Ach, she is ill. She does not know what she is doing. I have to help and protect her."

Three years later, in fact wo years after the divorce, during the very last discussion I ever had with her, she said that she no longer believed those accusations herself. However, she never said "sorry" and she never admitted that these false accusations had destroyed our marriage. Worse yet, during this very last discussion she proposed that I would come back home. She said she would forgive me for the relation I had with Hanne. I just laughed. What was there for her to forgive? That I had become a happy man, for example? Again much later, perhaps ten, twelve years later, I discovered that relative to her siblings and friends she had been a bit more careful with respect to these accusations of infidelity than I had hitherto assumed. She had talked about my frequent infidelities, but she had apparently never mentioned names. Only one case she spelled out in great detail, with name and circumstance. That was the affair with my sister-in-law Aletta. That accusation was also false, however, 100.00% false! This in fact she had also admitted during that one rare moment of truth. She didn't believe that one either anymore she said. Which did not stop her from repeating it time and again in her own circles.

How did I survive all this? Only because I pitied her, because I knew she was sick. Because I kept thinking of Ma who had psychologically warped this, her first-born. And because I still loved Lotte, very much so and for a very long time, even until after he divorce. Of course I asked Lotte at least a hundred times why she was doing all this to me. I never received the slightest answer. Whenever I insisted she would just turn on her heels and walk away. On a rare occasion she might say: "Because you have destroyed my life". When I next would press for details, on how I would have done that, then again I got no answer. She was my Princess and I was very proud of her. Now a change in that feeling crept in, very slowly without me noticing it. I noticed it for the first time one year after the divorce. Daughter Mieke got married so Lotte and I were the official witnesses. Lotte and I had agreed that we then would have a talk. Number one daughter was present at this meeting. Suddenly it came out of me: "The only thing that I really reproach you, Lotte, that is that you have destroyed my love for you". This was the moment that I realized that my marriage was really defunct, beyond repair. I must have known this inside me for some time; only now had I been able to say it in words. Lotte did not even react to this cry of despair. Even number one daughter caught the meaning: "Mama, listen to what this man is telling you", but Lotte started to rant and rave.

XLVIII

Intermission

All of a sudden the attack-of-the-32 stopped. Not that Lotte had no more candidates who could be promoted to *maitresse*. There were still some good, honest, faithful faculty wives who might have been slandered by Lotte. Why did she stop? I don't know. During this period a novel thought had been brewing though. Why was it that I had indeed been so true and faithful to Lotte? Why hadn't I taken on a nice jolly lady friend? Amongst my friends there were several who posed this question and not just secretly and silently. That might have saved my sanity and perhaps even my marriage, so they told me. It was not a question of my potency. There had been all kinds of seductive situations; I knew that the sexual fire still burned fiercely inside me. I have no answer but to suggest that I must have loved Lotte indeed very deeply. How boring, how *bourgeois*. Perhaps Lotte had reasoned from the absurd; a man with such a strong sexuality surely must have sex friends, that is unavoidable. Certainly when he gets no love at home. And that latter point Lotte knew better than anybody else. Surely there must have been women who could and would gladly give him the affection he so craved. OK, then I must have been an extraterrestrial being who achieved the humanly impossible. I was not very proud of this; I was made this way, I could not behave differently.

At one point I will tell all. Not to Lotte because she is not stupid and therefore she knows it all. She has long enough fought against the reality in order to know exactly what it is, at least in her lucid periods. There will come a time around when I will tell my children about all the evil that has been brought upon me. There will also come a time when I will tell all these good women who were slandered and whose honor was befouled by Lotte. But for the time being I said nothing and I did nothing. My way to protect Lotte and to protect my children. In so doing I wounded myself in a manner that was almost irreparable.

XLIX

Murder after all?

Afterwards I often thought of Hermann Göring, the boss of the German *Luftwaffe* in the second world war. He did not realize it at the time but he very nearly had won the Battle of Britain. The British Air Defense had only a few airworthy planes left. More Spitfires and Hurricanes were shot down than could be manufactured or repaired. Worse than this, there were only a few airfields left that were in serviceable condition. Precisely on this very critical point Göring managed to snatch defeat from the teeth of victory. He ceased the attacks on all airfields and switched to bombarding cities.

Why did Lotte change her tactics? There were indeed still enough good woman left to slander. On that moment I considered again whether I would call in the help from our family doctor. Lotte's behavior was irrational but not really dangerous and perhaps he could convince Lotte of accepting some form of treatment. He would most certainly recommend that she would see a psychiatrist, but Lotte just as surely would refuse that. Maybe some medication to calm her down? In the end I did not do it. Again.

I did already recount how Lotte at a certain night threw away her blankets and started to shout: "*Ik ga je vermoorden"*. The frightening aspect was not the threat itself but the fact that she said it in Dutch. Whenever Lotte became excited and began to scold she always did so in English. If she had screamed: "I am going to kill you", the threat would have been the same but not half as frightening. My ears sharpened up after this and I felt something like fear. Never before had she given physical support to her verbal threats. Only once had she slapped me in the face, but I had made it very clear to her that she should not ever do that again.

"If you ever do that again, I will slap you back, twice as hard and twice as many times", I said. And then she did it again. I reminded her of my earlier promise and while I stood right in front of her, I hit her as hard as I could, twice, once on the left cheek then on the right one. Lotte stood there, her body bending under the blows. She said nothing, uttered no sound. When I was finished she turned on her heels and went up the stairs to her office room. She stayed there for more than a day. Then I heard the sound of pots and pans from the kitchen. Half an hour later she called: "Dinner is ready". The subject was never mentioned again, but after that she never hit me ever again either. That was the first and also the last time that I ever used physical force against a woman. It taught me something about myself. With all my patience and my tolerance I apparently had also a limit, where even a dearly loved one could not transgress.

Now she wanted to kill me. Her 'show' she repeated several times. Each time she came a bit higher up the staircase, until she sat with her back against the bedroom door. Prior to that there had been a major screaming session, yelling, shouting, shrieking, screeching, screaming indeed, which made no sense. Lotte was not tall at all but she could produce an enormous voice, a roaring sound in fact. The terrifying aspect of it was that her voice acquired the actual timbre of Ma's voice. I could hear her rubbing against the bedroom door, most of the time that was it then. In the end she would get up, went downstairs for the ritual with the cutlery drawer and then she would come up again, into the bedroom, but without the knife. The situation was becoming very oppressive. When would she come in WITH the knife? It was in the air that this was going to happen, sooner or later. What could I then do? What COULD I do? I was afraid that I would fall asleep, because sometimes she sat against that door for 10-20 minutes. What would I do if all of sudden she would come running in? I had already concluded that Lotte would not kill me in cold blood. That she might easily have done earlier, in a moment that I was asleep. No, she would want to shout some last insults at me, before she would do the fatal stabbing. Lotte knew nothing about the art of fighting with a knife. To all likelihood she would come at me with the knife held high. The classical pose, but all wrong, because it would give me the chance to raise my arm and catch her thrust. I would then be wounded in my arm, but that was OK; Lotte then would never been convicted for murder, at most for attempted murder. Would I be able to find a bloodless solution? Perhaps I would. I prepared for her attack by pushing the top blanket against the bed board with my toes. At the same time I took the top of the blanket very tightly into my fists. The blanket then was tight. I hoped that I could catch her blow into that blanket or that I would be able to throw the blanket over her. That would even be better. My whole being concentrated on keeping her out of jail and also, if possible, out of a psychiatric hospital ward. For sure the last thing I would do in these circumstances was to call in professional help. As soon as my family doctor or whomever else could survey the situation, he would call in an ambulance with four strong male nurses, plus police back-up. I could only hope that this psychotic phase would pass. In the meantime there was not supposed to flow any blood, because then I would be forced to call the 911 alarm number and then all would be lost.

The attack did not weaken, to the contrary. I noticed a certain agitation behind the closed bedroom door. I heard how she got up and how she then let herself sag down. Her daytime behavior also became frightening. She then would look at me wide-open wild eyes and a distorted facial expression. Sometimes she said nothing, but mostly I heard her say: "*I hate you, I hate you, I hate you*".

I tried another technique. I went to the adjoining bedroom and tried to get some sleep there. Lotte became really very hysterical then. She banged on the door and begged me, no demanded that I should come out to return to the conjugal bed. She made so much noise that finally I gave in and indeed returned to my intended deathbed. Remarkable fact is that I never locked that bedroom door; she could just have walked in, but she did not even try it. Perhaps because it concerned the former bedroom of our number one daughter, a room that had been vacated in the meantime, but even so. Fodder again for a psychologist.

L

The Attack

When it finally happened it was still unexpected. I must have fallen into a light sleep, while Lotte was again sitting at the other side of the bedroom door. To be sure I had the blanket tightly between fists and toes, but would that turn out sufficient? Suddenly she stood next to me on my side of the bed, shouting, scolding and waving that knife in her right hand. She was going to kill me, so much she made clear. Even at this extreme moment not a word of explication why I had to be killed. I was the guilty party to everything in her life. Of what precisely was I guilty, Lotte? I admit that I love you, madly even, but that is no crime, is it? But there I lay, motionless, ready for action. I was watching every move of hers, all muscles tight and ready for the moment I could throw that blanket over her. I would have to subdue her and that might be difficult. The physical power of a crazed person can be enormous. Feverishly I was seeking for an opening, to hit her with something that would render her unconscious.

It was not needed. Without any further comment Lotte suddenly ran out of the room, back to the kitchen where I heard the now very familiar clattering of the knife. I realized that she now had crossed her Rubicon. Now nothing stood anymore between my body and her knife. The next time she would no longer hold back; then the knife would come at me. As after all previous attacks Lotte came back to the bedroom, without knife, with the full intention to go to sleep. This time something else ought to happen, I thought. We could not continue this way. I asked her: "Would it not be better, Lotte, if we would separate?" I meant divorce, naturally. Lotte turned to me:

"Fifty-fifty?"
"I agree"
"OK"

She turned around again and fell asleep. The next morning I was allowed to sleep in. It was almost noon before I reached the breakfast table in the kitchen. There I saw a very unusual spectacle. Lotte had emptied all drawers and all the cutlery and other kitchen hardware lay spread out on the kitchen table. Lotte was busily counting everything and entering the results into her laptop. The message could not be clearer.

Lotte never came back to that shortest of all night-time discussions in bed. The shouting, screaming, scolding, making accusations, waving around with that knife all of sudden had ceased. Like two auction masters we went through our possessions, writing down every item along with a street value. I went along with it, only semi-conscious, as if I was in a dream. With every item that was entered into the computer, another little piece of my dream was destroyed. However, no blood had been shed, thanks in part to my intervention. Now I had to live with this bloodless murder, the murder of my marriage. And the children knew nothing of it. That too was a plus. Neither did our social environment. That seemed a double plus too. These gains were temporary, though, and they were quickly turned around into my loss.

LI

Divorce

I have seen many movies which I have forgotten for 95%. Others left an indelible impression. *Divorce Italian Style* by Pietro Germi with Marcello Mastroianni in the lead role is one such unforgettable movie. Probably so un-forgotten because this movie seemed to lean very close on my own experiences. A very ill husband is being cared for in the conjugal bed. The entire family comes by to offer their best wishes overloading the bedroom with flowers, fruit baskets and what not. Unfortunately, the man does not really die and this becomes a nuisance, particularly in the view of his wife. In order to get her bed back the sick husband is first placed on a (narrow) hospital bed and brought to a much smaller room somewhere else in the house. That room too is soon needed for a daughter who is about to give birth to a child and a new (even smaller) room is found for our friend the husband. Eventually he ends up in a windowless closet. At about that time no one in the family knows whether he still lives and if so, where he might be.

I felt something like that when Lotte made it so clear that she wanted a divorce. On one side it was a relief.

The continual pestering, attacks and death threats was over. Lotte went through the entire home with pencil and pad and then everything was digitally entered. I had a little input, mostly because every item had to be appraised and be given a street price, the value it would bring in an auction sale or at a garage sale. We both engaged a lawyer and a concept separation act was drawn up. It gave me something to do; almost on the overdrive I did the needed things in an almost mechanistic fashion. The other side was that I felt strangely empty. An enormous sense of loss, of having lost came over me. I felt beaten and I had, yes, also that feeling of having failed. Forty long years I had put myself in the service of this women, fighting at every turn against the demons that threatened her and us. I had failed, that much was clear. Our marriage was shattered and there was no glue capable of mending it again. It was over, even when I didn't know why. That was the other thing that kept coming back at me again and again. My marriage, our marriage was in tatters and I had no idea how that had happened. Lotte never gave a *clou.* Her verbal abuse had ceased and instead we had civilized talks about the price of this or that piece of furniture. I walked around, I answered questions but in another sense I wasn't even there. I had the feeling that I would die very soon. I thought that my immune system was weakened to the point that the next cold would kill me. Neither was I there with my brains when it came to negotiating. I was thinking: "Please, take it. Take it all, soon I will be dead anyway". Lotte used these circumstances to very expertly strip me naked. In a certain sense I was co-responsible for this. I should not have given her the chance; I had lost all fighting spirit. The story of the finalizing of the divorce is a story of hundreds of battles, small and large; I lost almost all of them. Lotte did not show the slightest pity; she must really have hated me deeply because she grabbed without any consideration. Therefore no count-by-count report but just a few examples.

My stamp collection had a street value of about $4,000. That is what a dealer might give for it. Lotte knew, however, that I had insured the collection for $33,000, but that is replacement value, the money needed to replace the collection should it ever get lost. I offered to let the collection be appraised by a stamp dealer, but Lotte would not agree. "Those are all friends of yours. They will value it to your advantage". No, she demanded that he collection came for the full $33, 000 on the list, and I was stupid enough to agree to that. Worse even, I agreed to buy the collection from the list for the full $33,000, money that I even didn't have. How stupid can you be? Again my thinking was, I am dying anyway, I want to enjoy these stamps for the last little time I had in this life. Actually I had nothing else left and these stamps had always been kind to me. I should have refused to buy hem, actually such personal things like collections, jewelry, books are usually kept outside the division. If I had been a bit smarter I would have said: "OK Lotte, I don't want these stamps. You think they are worth $33, 000, you may buy them from me for half that price." Failing that, the divorce judge would finally have to rule on the undivided active. In the end I sold my half of the home to Lotte; now suddenly a friend of Lotte was allowed to do the appraisal. Naturally the amount was ridiculous, but I agreed nevertheless. I expected to receive half of that sales price but Lotte was ahead of me. She thought up all kinds of deductions; I received only $20,000 for half my home, a capital 5-level house with five bedrooms, four bathrooms, a dark room, a bar, an entertainment room and still a deep cellar.

The end result was as follows. When I had paid all my bills and I had moved to the Netherlands with a table, four chairs, two cupboards, a few book shelves, a narrow steel spring bed and two easy chairs my entire wealth was -$12,000. Yes, you are reading correctly. I was technically bankrupt; I owned minus $12,000. I was 64, at the end of a life time of high level work which had left me with less than nothing. No home, no car, no money in the bank, no pension, only some old furniture and debts. Yes, plus that stamp collection. Lotte had a capital home free on her name with 90 % of all the furniture and furnishings, a beautiful car (Oh, yes, I forgot to mention, the Volvo 740 Turbo, only a few years old, had also gone to her) and tons of money in the bank. I am running ahead of myself again. Of course, there was that Legal Document of Separation; every little tea spoon was in it but also such important things like alimentation and the partition of my pension Fund. It only needed to be confirmed by a judge and then it would have become law. The document had been signed by Lotte and me and by our respective lawyers. However, Lotte never stuck to it; in fact she did her utmost to prevent any judge from ever seeing this document. I could not force her. I had hoped and expected that a judge would see to a fair distribution; I knew full well that I was in no shape to look after my own interests. As it happened no judge ever presided over the distribution of goods and Lotte went her stealing way unimpeded.

The day after that document had been signed and had become effective, I departed for the Netherlands. I was truly desperate, I needed to get away from this 'place of delict'. I needed rest in order to think about the past events. There was only a tiny problem; I had no money whatsoever. The incredible things is that I then borrowed $5,000 from Lotte to pay for this 'holiday'. At the time it did not occur to me as strange that I had nothing and that she had everything. Later, this generosity on my part was used by Lotte's family, her sister Betty in the forefront, that this 'proved' how guilty I must have felt. No normal being would ever do such a thing so it must have been my sense of guilt. Rarely have I seen or heard a more beautiful example of Marxist-Leninist dialectics.

One of the first people I visited in the Netherlands was this Betty. I had a number of interesting presents for her. Or better said, for her spider collection. With Betty I had always had a very friendly and positive relation. My presents were extensively admired and then it was lunch time. After lunch the atmosphere became suddenly nasty and even ghastly and this without any warning or cause. The words "Lotte" or "divorce" were not used at all but suddenly I was made out to be a sod. Then she said: "I would like you now to leave my home". How can you treat someone like this without uttering a single accusation? It is a rare gift and the Ten Brink family appeared to have patent rights to it. Betty's husband who had been witnessing the scene, sneaked out of the room, without even looking at me. Apparently it got too much for him too. Once more I got kicked into the stomach. There I had been good and generous and loving to their sibling Lotte and now this! By the way, it became clear here how Lotte had betrayed me once more. Before I had departed and had said my farewells to Lotte, she had asked me very urgently that I would tell no-one what had transpired between the two of us in our marriage. Especially not to anyone of her family, she had added. Now it was evident that Lotte had extensively talked to her family, blaming me entirely. I had promised to keep my mouth shut and I kept my promise, for more than ten years. When pressed I only said that I was innocent, that I had in fact no idea why I was divorced. And that was the truth. What might be the reason? What had I done wrong? Lotte had told me nothing and for myself I could not imagine anything. I had yet to learn that even my question was entirely wrong. Of course, I had done nothing wrong, that was not the point. It turned about who I was. I, with all my knowledge about world history should have known better and most certainly sooner. The Jews had also not done anything wrong that justified their murder. They were gassed because of whom they were, not because of anything they did.

LII

Leaving Home

Those six months in the Netherlands didn't do me much good. I still did not find answers to the many questions I had. I could not reach any decisions and I did not know what to do in the future. Except that I had to get away from that beautiful home that was so full of my dreams, away from Lotte, away from everything, far away. At the very least I wanted no more knifing incidents. Friends in the Netherlands were good to me. I had several addresses where I was welcome, where I could stay as long as I wished and where I perhaps could talk a bit about my sadness. That particular Summer was hot and long. I slept a lot and lazied about in the garden of my friends. The only decision that I reached was that I wanted out of my home as quickly as possible. And that now was my next blunder.

I came home and the first thing I noticed was that it was empty. Lotte was not there. I soon found out that she was staying with number one daughter. When I next got Lotte on the phone, she dumped a fresh carload of dirt all over me. Again accusations of infidelity. That really shocked me; we were at that moment legally separated, so what did she want? Furthermore it was Lotte who had destroyed the marriage, not I, so what was the idea? That I would still forever stay single? Besides, the accusations were again false. If there was anything that I was totally not ready for, then it was a new relation. It soon became clear what Lotte wanted. She wanted me out of the home and until that happened she would not come home. I should have said: "Fine! Great!" Against the strong advice of my lawyer I agreed to leave. I should have just stayed for at least one year. Then the divorce would become definitive in the Province of residence and then the division of the goods would also automatically be regulated. At that time the home was still mine as well as Lotte's so I could certainly never be removed. I had enough of all the verbal abuse. I found a little apartment some 800 km away; to me that seemed to be far enough removed from Lotte so that I would be safe. I rented a small truck, loaded a few belongings into it and drove off. Again through a snowy and ice cold Canada. That other December trip through Canada was so recent, yet it seemed far away. At the other occasion we were a happy family singing along in that old Volvo. Now I was alone; no wife anymore, children far away. I had just committed the greatest blunder of my life. Correction: the greatest but one, of course.

LIII

Depression

For the third time now I had fallen prey to depression and I knew it. Right through a maximum dose of Prozac I had only one wish and that was to disappear from this valley of tears called earth as soon as possible. When you wake up in the morning and you begin to cry because you don't know how to get through the day, then you are heavily depressed. Three or four times I stood on that little balcony, looking down fourteen floors. Why didn't I jump? I will tell you. That was because every time I thought of my children. Not only would they have to scrape me up from that sheet of concrete, as a figure of speech, I would certainly have loaded an enormous guilt feeling on their shoulders. I knew enough about deeply depressed people to know that eventually they do jump. A courageous colleague of mine had done it right the first time; he had jumped from a tower flat that was a-building.

However, I was saved or rescued you might say and this happened in a very unusual manner. On a certain morning I sat in the coffee room of our apartment, when Anneliese entered. She told us that she just had returned from the burial of her best lady friend, the only one with whom she could speak her mother's tongue, the German language. I could not contain myself and said: *"Liebe Anneliese, weisst du dann nicht dass ich auch Deutsch sprechen kann?"* Or: "Dear Anneliese, don't you know that I also speak German?" She fell just about in my arms and began to cry. Soon I began to understand why she reacted so emotionally. Anneliese was born on the wrong side of the river Oder. Her town was given to the Polish, when that country was moved some 100 km Westwards. She, her family and countless others suddenly became DPs or Displaced Persons with no home to go back to. When she turned eighteen, she applied for immediate emigration to Canada and that she had been granted. Totally alone and by herself, without any knowledge of the English language she had arrived in Canada. She had asked for Guelph, a town in Ontario, because somewhere she had heard that in that town there were many ethnic Germans. In that way her Canadian adventure had started and now she was still in Canada. Many adventures later, and also many men later, because Anneliese was not only strikingly beautiful but also very naïve. Her latest marriage had failed when her husband stole all her money and had left her alone in a kind of slave hut, that you still may find in Canada as shelter for the transient agricultural workers. Yes, such things also happen in that beautiful Canada. Then she had her first attacks of depression and the wish to die. Then somebody had helped her and now she was determined to help me. She pulled me away from the window. "No way that humping from balcony. Come here I tell you what to do. On your knees and then we pray together." I protested that I did no longer believe in God because if he existed he was a bastard for letting me suffer so much and abandoning me. "Doesn't matter. On your knees. Perhaps He sent me to you". That was a clever thought and so we began: *"Unser Vater der ist im Himmel. Our Father Thou art in heaven. Uw naam worde geheiligd"*. In three languages we stumbled through the half-forgotten prayer. Suddenly a restful feeling began to flow through my system. Anneliese grabbed my hand: "You see! Now it will get good". Anneliese would come to the rescue a few more times; we would hold hands and pray. Anneliese saved my life. Tragically, our friendship came to an abrupt ending. Through her I had gotten to know the German 'colony' in our city. A collection of ethnic Germans who had managed to escape alive from the second world war. One should perhaps remember that Germany was reduced to a much smaller area after the Peace of Versailles in 1918-1920. About ten million ethnic Germans then lived outside the new German territory. These diaspora Germans were living in places like Bessarabia, Bukovina, the Vojvodina, Lithuania, the Wolga basin, Poland, White Russia and Czechia. So I had made acquaintance with Hans who as Sudeten-German was still grateful to Adolf Hitler for having liberated him from those awful Czechs. He then had immediately volunteered and had lived through the war as a member of an elite German paratroop regiment. Now he had contracted cancer of the liver; five weeks later he was dead and his burial was organized. Together with Anneliese I sat on the last bench in the Lutheran church. While the German *Pfarrer* was giving his eulogy, Anneliese's hand had landed between my legs, where she began to massage my crown jewels. I was absolutely not in for such an activity. I pulled the keys of her car out of my pocket, threw them to her, got up and departed for a very long walk home.

After about a year I began to get used to my new environment and my new life. I became active once again. On the advice from Esther I began to write, partly as therapy, but soon I began to enjoy writing. I joined a local writers group and wrote poetry, short stories and what not. I noticed that people liked my literary contributions, especially when I wrote stories about the Old World.

LIV

Sandra

And then Sandra walked into my life. It was Old & New and in the coffee room a dance had been organized. Not that I wanted to dance, but you know, sitting alone in your room is not much fun either. Sandra had arrived in our complex only one hour earlier. Another victim, this time of a man who followed her everywhere in order to beat her up. Sandra was young and really beautiful. Later I heard that she was half Scottish and half Apache Indian. We danced a bit and soon we were in deep discussion about everything. About life in particular. Sandra was rather intelligent and she used me happily to try out her sometimes extreme opinions. I thought that I was rather black and gloomy, but Sandra made of me a very rational, pros and contras weighing man. We became friends, of course, without ever getting intimate. The friendship ended on an angry note, on the evening before my departure and return to the Netherlands. Sandra had invited me to her room (wow, that had never happened before) and I, the sod, had said: "Thank you, but no thank you". That was an insult to Sandra and she did not understand. Evidently this had never happened to her before. In her bewilderment she scolded me from top to bottom: "Now, what kind of man was I? She offered herself in friendship and I had the nerve to say no?" Much later, when reflecting about it I thought what a son-of-a-bitch I had been. At long last some affection is offered to you, from the heart, and you refuse. You always wanted that and see now! After my manhood had been so deeply wounded, the scars from the castration by Lotte were still too sensitive. I still was not up to a new love life. However, I must add that I was proud about my refusal of Sandra. Not for the content of it; rather because I realized that a new "Me" had been born. I existed once more as a real person. In fact I was on my way to become once more a man. Curious that in order to become man I had to abandon my manhood.

And the latter was alive and well, considering also the enormous erection I got immediately after having rejected Sandra. I have Sandra never seen again, but I do think of her sometimes. How would she look now? Probably even more beautiful than she was then, with that acquiline nose line turning into her long eyebrows. And then those apple cheeks, now replaced by the sharp lines of her jaws flowing to her high cheek bones. If she would see me now, she would for sure first curse me stiff for five minutes and then come into my arms. Then we would look into each other's eyes again, she into my orangy-brown ones that she thought so beautiful and I into her deep black pools. And then perhaps .... No, then absolutely we would give each other that tenderness that then had not been possible.

LV

Hanne

Two years after my divorce I went again to the Netherlands, for a holiday and perhaps for something more. I wanted to find out whether or not I might migrate back to the country of my birth. My lust for life had also returned in another way; I wanted to find a new partner for life. Indeed, I had come a long distance since those dramatic balcony scenes. In Canada finding a new partner would be difficult. No marriage ever again for me; I was cured entirely and forever of that idea. However, in that conservative Canada no decent woman would live with a man without getting married. Perhaps for a little while, one or two years at most, but then there had to be marriage. If not, then the woman would conclude that her friend was not serious and was forever on the look-out for other women, other birds. In the Netherlands the situation was totally different. There they had something called a LAT relation, with LAT standing for Living Apart Together. That was precisely what I was looking for. I did not want to be a 'bird watcher', but neither did I think that an official piece of paper would be helpful. That would undoubtably give rise to problems. Apart from that, Lotte kept refusing to sign the official divorce papers so officially we were still married!

I had also a date with a widow. I had met Hanne and her husband in the Netherlands two years before, in March, during a meeting of the "Child Welfare" collectors club. This means the annual postage stamps, picture postcards, posters, door stickers, everything connected with that annual event. I had bought some door stickers from her, but she had more at home, she told me. "Make a list of what you need or want and then I will look what I have for you". So, we exchanged addresses; it was Fall before I wrote her. "I don't know if you will remember me......". I got an immediate reply. She wrote that she had done nothing about stamps and collecting during the entire Summer. In June her husband had made a bicycle trip with some friends on the heath. He became ill, fell off his bike and had died on the spot. Now she would start looking for me, because that would be a welcome distraction. A correspondence ensued, quickly followed by phone calls and then very quickly an invitation to come and see her. I could stay at her place she said, during my next visit to the Netherlands.

And I had thought: "Well, well, Hanne, can you really do that? Widow and then inviting a single man to come and stay with you? I knew that she lived right at the center of the Dutch Bible Belt. I did not know at the time that Hanne belonged to the upper ten of her village. She lived in a big home right opposite the Dutch Reformed church. She was member of that congregation, supported that Church also financially but the minister better not think that he could tell her anything. One of her habits was to bike to the tennis courts around ten or eleven o'clock on Sunday morning. She did that in her tennis outfit, inclusive a very short shorts showing her more than beautiful bare legs. And that in a black-stockings community? Nobody who would dare to comment on that. She made also no point about inviting an unattached man to come and sleep in her home. The Dutch saying goes: "merchant, preacher", meaning quite literally that money is more important than God. Hanne was rich and she knew the perks that came with that.

In the plane I had thought carefully about it: "Three days at most, Gus, that is the decent limit." The rest is history. I never left. We fell for each other like teenagers perhaps do. Without thinking, without any reserve. I went back for a few weeks to clean out my Canadian existence and to send some belongings to the Netherlands. In Nijkerk I rented a little home so that I had my own *pied á terre* but for most of the time I lived, ate and slept with Hanne. This did not do any good to my divorce proceedings. The new lawyer I had hired turned out an oaf, although he advertised divorce as his specialty. Lotte succeeded in squeezing more and more money and concessions out of me but she refused to sign the final divorce document. I could have forced the issue by simply stopping her alimentary payments. In that case she would have been forced to go to a judge and then everything would quickly have been finalized. Once more I detested this kind of warfare to the extent that I rather gave in to Lotte. Finally I made her an offer she could not refuse. Rather than paying her alimentation I offered her half of my pension fund. That was extremely generous, considering all she had already gotten, far more than any judge would ever award her. On the advice of her lawyer she accepted the deal. She received promptly the money, but nothing else happened. Lotte still refused to sign the divorce papers! And that had been a *conditio sine quoi non*. I had to threaten to recoup the money, then others interfered and finally she signed, only five years after the date. You see, now she could claim (and did so) that she was dead set against divorce and that Gus had forced her! How clever, how sly, how totally rotten.

Why had I so strongly insisted on her signing those papers? To begin with I hoped in that way to gain some rest, since Lotte would no longer be able to contact me and make more demands. Also the marriage was broken and there was no hope that it could be repaired. Lotte had even managed to kill my love for her. I also would like to be freed of my daily fears that her murderous psychotic attacks would return. Finally, suppose I would return to her, she would do well to recognize that I would no longer hesitate. In no time flat she would end up in the same psychiatric ward she had so long been trying to avoid. Even at this stage I did not want that. Not for her, not for the children. But I would do it. To save my own soul.

Now Lotte could walk away with the story that I had wanted the divorce. In the end Lotte also walked away with about three quarters of our material wealth, leaving me behind in semi poverty. I don't even count here the approximately five million dollar in missed income, missed by her doings. And all that because I had loved this woman too much, way too much. She really had become my *femme fatale*.

LVI

Jacob

Hanne and I were two very different personalities. Small wonder then that now and then frictions would arise. Then we looked each other into the eyes and then we knew it again. God had arranged this for us, that on his riper age we would find our fulfilling in each other. We both had this feeling very strongly. Had Hanne then had such a bad marriage? "He was my best friend" Hanne said of him. He adored her and he did everything to please her. Everything she asked for and even when she had not yet asked for it. Problems with the maid? He solved it. Educate their sons? He took care of that too, and Hanne had never occupied herself with that. Her big great love he had never been, though. She too?! She had married him because he was so persistent and because she wanted to get away from the oppressive atmosphere at her parental home. She came from a severe Reformed family with her father and grandfather being very active in that 'black stockings' Church. On one occasion she had come home with a Jewish boy friend, but he wasn't even allowed to come in. Yet, he was from a distinguished family of Barristers and Judges. However, the Bible said: "His blood may come over us and all our offspring" and Hanne had been instructed to never see this David again. In those circles I, being a Roman Catholic young man, would not even have gotten as far as their garden fence. To be honest, in those years I did never look at Protestant girls. I avoided them at all cost. Not even for a stroll, a movie or a cup of coffee.

Jacob did carry a biblical name but mainly he was not so severe in his religion. He was member of a Netherlands Reformed Evangelical Church where they would sing a lot in a special drawn-out moaning way. Jacob had money and that counted for more. He was a successful business man in the local Nijkerk world and Hanne sort of liked him. After a weekend in Brussels (as a try-out; again one of those sneaky Calvinist habits) she had agreed in an engagement and at the beautiful age of twenty one she had married this Jacob. In rapid succession she had born him three sons. She had enjoyed becoming a mother and all these baby things. Even so, she had told her Jacob that she thought enough is enough. She meant that she did not want any more sex with him. When I heard that story my immediate reaction was: "Were you not afraid that he would go to the whores?" "Ah, if he had such needs he should go ahead, provided he would do it very secretive and discrete".

Her reply was even more revealing than the facts themselves. In the local Gentlemen's Society he had let get off steam and I also heard about that: "Deflowered, inseminated, thanks and no, thank you".

The story made me think about my own adventures in the Red District. No, not what you think, but I liked to talk to the Ladies and sometimes I was even allowed to take pictures. Nowadays this is no fun anymore. What to do with a gal from Guatamala, who barely speaks three words Dutch and who even in her own language barely can read or write? In my younger years that was very different. They were all Holland girls, here and there with a pimp, but mostly 'small business'. At those days you could still talk with the Ladies, who did it mostly to earn a living. Often they had a child somewhere in an expensive boarding school and that had to be paid somehow, true or not? Many of them came from respectable families, had received good education, sometimes even University degrees. Next they were thrown out by their loving parents, when they had gotten pregnant without bring married. Yeah, what can you then do? I remember how busy the ladies were on Thursdays. That was the day of the weekly horse market in Zwolle and the Frisian farmers flocked to that. Except that quite a number of them took the wrong boat that took them to Amsterdam from Lemmer or Stavoren. As a matter of fact, the Monday mornings were also busy times with all those small business men from the Veluwe. With their shops closed they had to go to Amsterdam to buy new supplies. I once asked whether there would be a danger that they would then accidentally meet their minister of the cloth. The reply was breathtaking: "No, because these would come only on Saturday mornings".

Hanne was sufficiently loyal to never have taken a lover. Instead she just day-dreamt of that unknown Great Lover. In that frame of mind it is understandable that she saw it as a Message from Heaven when my letter had fallen on her door mat. Once I asked Hanne whether she had not perhaps seen something Freudian in the two big hobbies of her husband Jacob. In his garden he had a large aviary where he was breeding parakeets. His second great love was growing cacti in a large glass house that he had constructed. No, she had never thought about that, but on occasion she had felt like a bird that was kept in a golden cage. She was allowed to get out once and a while, provided she would always return to her little cage. And no, after the birth of her third son, she had never let him get close. As a prickly pear. Another poor sod.

LVII

Hanne's Death

We were very happy with each other and we really thought we would be together for the next 20-30 years; unfortunately our Creator had different plans. Because Hanne was going to die. Not suddenly but very slowly, more or less chokingly. It started with me noticing that she had problems finishing her sentences and that she had concentration problems with playing bridge. She handled that very cleverly so that nobody, except me of course, would notice. A neurologist and a neurosurgeon said that it was nothing. She was certainly not dementing. That I also knew. During a trip to Canada a befriended psycho therapist had reacted alarmingly. She was not fooled and had impressed upon us several times to ask for an MRI once we got home. The neurologist initially would not oblige but in the end he had given in. Because it was indisputably clear that Hanne had speech problems and he had no explanation for it. The MRI showed a large black spot in her brain, right where the speech function is located. Exploratory surgery revealed an incurable and inoperable tumor, of which she would most certainly die. Hanne by that time was too far gone to understand. Soon she was no more than a child of age two, and not long thereafter she fell into a coma.

Hanne died a lonely death with only me and a nurse being present. Her sons had given me very clear instructions; they were only to be warned after a medical doctor had certified her death. The nurse had awakened me saying that the moment was there. Suddenly her eyes opened. Those eyes had been closed for at least two weeks and now they were there again, those bright blue sparkling eyes. Did she recognize me? I spoke to her but I don't know if any of it got through to her. But she looked and looked for perhaps twenty long minutes. Then she closed her eyes and she was gone. I kissed her on her mouth and said my fare well to her. *Vaja con Dios.* We will meet again in the other world.

My loved one was dead, after almost five years of a very intense relation. This was the woman who threw her arms around my neck and told me that she loved me: "Gus, I love you". I was then 64 years of age and that was the first time in my life that I had heard those heavenly words.

A feeling of an enormous sadness rose up in me. However, it was tempered at every turn by my feeling of gratefulness for having had these years with her. With her I was truly for the first time a complete man, because she answered my manly love and made me feel that I made her happy. With her I came to realize that making a woman happy was my true vocation in life. I had tried it before but now I had finally succeeded. It had been only for a limited time, but I had tasted it. It gave me strength and a desire to find it again.

Hanne's death left me with a twofold problem. Staying in Nijkerk, in that suffocating reformed community, that was out. But before leaving I had to find out where to. Back to Canada was a clear option. That was where my children were living although that was barely a good point. The three daughters lived thousands of kilometers apart, so a true family life was not realistic. As a matter of fact from Amsterdam-Schiphol I was closer to number one daughter in Toronto than, say, from Vancouver. It was also quicker and considerably cheaper. Canada is some 10,000 km wide from one extreme to the other. In the Netherlands *Omas* don't understand that: "Why are you not going to live with your children?" How often would they visit their own child if that child was living in Vladivostok?

The other point was even worse. During my life with Hanne, my ex Lotte had been no problem. I really thought that I had overcome that divorce but that turned out to be a mistake. The images of a knife-wielding Lotte began to haunt me again. The un-addressed pain came shooting to the surface like a cork in the water. With it the problems with my children. They had behaved civilized towards Hanne but they clearly did not accept any more. With the exception of Mieke, our youngest. Mieke had never forgotten the support she had gotten from me and so she kept believing in papa, even though she did not know what had happened. The other two did not know that either but the very close proximity of my slandering ex-wife they had not been able to withstand. As a matter of interest, how could they have known, what was truth and what was slander?

I had never given them any details and in fact they also never would have listened to me. They blankly told me to 'shut up' when I told them as little as letting them know that I was very sad. But to their mother they never said that. Of course Astrid should never have been committed the ultimate stupidity of inviting her mother to come and live in her village. Number one daughter had exceeded that by a whispering campaign that I was mad because of the Prozac and that I therefore should be locked up in an institution. During my time with Hanne I didn't care about these shenanigans, because it seemed utterly irrelevant. Suddenly this became a different story. Of course, I wanted good contacts with my children. Fat chance.

LVIII

On to The Hague

To make a long story short, I decided NOT to return to Canada. That was a difficult decision and it had taken several years. It appeared to me that it was not a good idea to take any important, life-changing decision so shortly after Hanne's death. I had to catch my breath and digest the past happenings. It was clear to me that I should not stay in Nijkerk, but the question was: where to? The Netherlands had one major trump card. Nowhere else in the world will you find such world-level cultural activities so close together as in this *Randstad Holland,* the area roughly defined by the great cities Amsterdam, the Hague, Rotterdam, Utrecht and the other old cities within this circle. The best symphony orchestra in the world, plus some more excellent orchestras and other ensembles large and small, opera, exhibitions, it is all there. And all that within one hour of travel if you lived a bit centrally. You may wonder how this is possible in a country that once was defined by Descartes as a land of frumps and boors. Question of distinction between civilization and culture? After Hanne's death I more and more took in the cultural life that the Netherlands had to offer. Ultimately this became the deciding factor. I decided to stay in the Netherlands, but I would move to the Hague as an ideal central location. I also decided to go and visit Canada once a year. New problems arose with that plan. Daughter Astrid managed to keep me out of her home for eleven years. I was never invited and whenever I tentatively invited myself there was always a reason why it could not happen. I did see her a couple of times, when she visited Europe or when she visited Mieke while I happened to be there too. Or we met in a holiday farm or in a couple of bungalows next to a beautiful lake. Never in her home, in her town. During the same period I was only once welcomed by number one daughter. It was painfully obvious; papa Gus had to be avoided like the black plague. Naturally I was partly to blame for this myself. I had promised Lotte to say nothing and I was still keeping that promise. It was also clear that this promise for which she had beseeched me had never been respected by Lotte herself. How long would I maintain this? When are you going to love yourself a bit? This I had heard now several times by a number of people. After ten years I decided that it had been enough now. I would never demand from my children that they should love me, but a little bit of respect, yes I thought I deserved that much. No, that was not it either. It was the injustice of it all that I disliked. I decided to write a 'red letter' to my daughters. "If you do that you will lose them definitely and completely", I was warned by my friends. As it was I had already lost them and worse, I had lost them in dishonor. Let me make clear that Mieke got a quite different letter. I informed her of what I was planning to write to the other two and I thanked her for the support she had always given me.

But the essence was nevertheless that I was breaking a silence that had lasted ten years. I told them all that the divorce from their mother had caused me great sadness, that somewhere I felt co-responsible although I could not describe how and where I was to blame.

I wrote: "Let it be clear though that nowhere, absolutely nowhere am I guilty of anything. The divorce was 100% engineered by your mother. I have done all I could to stop her but in the end I had to give in. Your mother has circulated great stories about my infidelity; in the years after the divorce she herself has recanted them all. Now there is not a single reason left that I know about why she did destroy this marriage. Perhaps she does not know herself; in any case she has never told me. I have asked her hundreds of times what I did wrong but she never gave a concrete reason. In case you might doubt, ask your mother if she can confirm this."

I also complained about the uncivil way I had been treated by my oldest two daughters the last ten years. I referred to the Ten Commandments where it says you have to honor your father and your mother, and why it was that they honored their mother but not me. Why they treat me like a despicable scabby dog. To number one daughter I had an extra request namely to stop with her slanderous accusations of incest. I had heard that quite recently she had complained to her two sisters that she had acquired a lifelong trauma because of that incest by her father. And that while long ago she had declared to me, to her mother and to others, that nothing untoward had ever happened. Now she had done it again and that had been perhaps the decisive reason for writing this dunning letter. Why would I go on letting myself being abused? I wrote those letters as real paper letters sent by the mail in an envelope with a stamp and address. An e-mail letter can be clicked away in a second; with a paper letter that is a bit more difficult. Number one daughter initially did not react at all. After half a year she phoned me! There was a Congress in Amsterdam that Fall and she was contemplating attending.

"Am I welcome? And can I take my little son Gregor with me?"

"Of course!"

Gregor was twelve by now and a week with a twelve-year old grandson may be very nice indeed. Of course not one word was said about my letter, not then and not during their stay. She was in fact as sweet as can be, but I also had a good opportunity to observe my grandson Gregor. I found him a rather scary boy and the way his mother appeared to bring him up I didn't like either. However, I kept my mouth shut. I thought every time: "Look here now, this is how the fourth generation psychotic is created". Anything else I had not expected, to say he truth. This daughter was totally unable to say "sorry". I have never heard that from her mouth. Not once. This she does not have from her father.

Astrid did it worse, actually. She phoned me and came with a proposal: "Papa, it does not matter if you did or did not do certain things. Can we not just continue as before? And I will invite you to come and visit us." Ah, splendid! In that way I remain forever under that cloud of suspicion. So like, perhaps he did it, perhaps he didn't, but let us not talk about it. Of course, I refuse that categorically. I am 100% innocent and that has to be acknowledged by you all and implanted firmly into your brains. And in the mean time I have paid a terrible price. Refunds anyone? Why is it that you refuse to seek either a denial or a confirmation from your mother? Would you think it so terrible if you would find out that your father is indeed entirely innocent?

Astrid did not give up and maintained her plan. I had heard more than enough and I told her that I wanted nothing to do with her, not now and not soon thereafter. In spite of this quarrel I would say that Astrid always was a good kid. Her main problem is that she is a very poor communicator. That is mainly because of her silent withdrawn nature; she has never learned how to speak in the sense of being open in listening and responding. This had cost her already career opportunities but it also means that she has a fear of discussing problems. And if and when she does speak, she lacks experience and will therefore make mistakes. After which she hides even more in her cocoon. Sometimes I would like to break open her mouth, but that really does not work and so I remain silent too. In this way a long period of radio silence ensued; about which I felt that Astrid would feel as badly as I did. Picking up the phone and start a real conversation with her dad? Are you out of your mind? Never a true word shall be spoken.

LIX

After the Dunning Letter

Still I wasn't entirely unhappy with the results following my letter. I thought that the problem with Astrid could be solved. With her it was not that she wasn't willing; it was her inexperience in solving people problems. And perhaps fear. How could I break through that? And then the reaction of number one daughter; could I be so happy with that? Entirely following her age-old script she had said nothing and had sailed straight past all problems. It was absolutely necessary that I broke through that wall. And how was I to do that without damaging my relation with my third daughter Mieke?

Already some 10-12 years earlier Esther, my excellent psychotherapist, my person of trust, my lady friend, had proposed to me that I should write up my experiences around my divorce. At the time I had started with that right away. It worked indeed as a therapy, but in the years thereafter I had continued the effort. I had also discovered that I could not write about certain matters. The death threats by Lotte and her knife for a long time sat too closely under the skin, too closely to be able to write about it in an objective fashion. In the end that episode too was set down in words and sentences.

At that point they were a collection of almost twenty essays about the various phases of my life with emphasis on my forty years with Lotte. They had never been intended any differently than FOR MY EYES ONLY. It was a somewhat motley collection with no sense of chronology; the episodes had been written down in apparent arbitrary order. Being meant for me alone, I had been very open and direct in my description of persons and events and interpretations thereof. Everything was there, including matters I had never discussed with anyone. Intimate details about Lotte, but also about myself and my daughters.

I decided to send this bunch of essays to my children. After the 'hot' letter, which had been a partial success now these personal experiences and reflections. It would be impossible for them to get around these. I would still not require from them to take sides, but after thirteen years of silence they should hear my side of the story. I did realize that it was a risky undertaking. All of a sudden my children would be exposed to all kinds of details from my married life. Would they be turned off by so much new facts and truths? In addition they themselves figured in many of these essays. Would they be able to accept these analytical stories by their father? There was no way to predict their reactions. I waited until there was an opportunity to speak personally to each of them.

I started my Odyssey with Mieke. Logical, because with her I always had maintained a good relation. I was really on pins and needles. I decided to first approach Mieke's husband John. John was also still a young person but he had already seen much of the seamy side of society working with junks, drunks and assorted homeless. I showed him a single chapter, although it was perhaps the worst one, describing Lotte's murder plans. "Will Mieke be able to cope with this?" I asked John. He replied that he would like to see more of my writings and I gave him the entire stack. He stayed on the safe side, saying that Mieke was a strong person, but this was about her mother, whom she did love. Finally he said: "Just do it, otherwise we will never know". I then gave the entire stack of essays to Mieke, explaining what it was and why I was now doing this. I warned her that many of the details might be shocking to her and that in no way I was forcing her to read it. Mieke replied that she would like to read it all and she disappeared with the papers into her bedroom. No explosion followed. In fact I got an interesting, unexpected reaction from her. There was much, she said, that reminded her of her own psychological problems, such as the depressions she had suffered. Some matters from her own life now had become clear. She left it at that; not much perhaps, but I was elated by her reaction. For one, she had not kicked me out of her home, but instead had given some measured remarks, not about it all, but about certain facets that had also touched on her life. Encouraged I traveled on to the holiday farm, where I would meet the other two daughters.

As soon as I saw them without presence of others, I showed them the two envelopes, that I wanted to give to them. I explained what was in them and asked them to please read the contents. I did not ask for comments,

I added; it was sufficient if they would take note of my side of the divorce question. Number one daughter said immediately that she would read it at a later time, at home. Fine, no problem. Astrid told me a day later that she had read it all, together with her husband, but that she preferred not to react. That was fine too. However, number one daughter had lied! When I stood at the Greyhound bus, ready for my travels back to the Netherlands, she came to me and said that she had read it all that very same night she had received it. I had already felt that the two daughters had talked about it with each other. They both were nice to me the remaining days, but no further comments came forward.

I knew it, I knew it. Number one daughter would never give in. Three months later a phone call from number one daughter. Apparently she had gotten increasingly concerned about whom might have read that document. I told her that a few professionals had read the entire collection and that she should just trust me that I would be careful. She tried to find out which persons had read certain chapters, but I did not provide any further details. I did mention that I had remained silent for ten years, and that therefore I was well used to maintaining silence. Then she tried another tack. Was I aware that everything I had written were my personal opinions? I replied that those things I presented as facts were verifiable and that where I gave opinions these always were labeled as such. It was clear that something was abrewing. The explosion came shortly afterwards. From Mieke I had received no further reactions, except that she sent lots of photos from her, indeed very photogenic, daughter. Astrid was very sweet. She had seen that my slippers were worn and she sent new ones, made by Indians from deer leather lined with sheep fur. Nice and warm against the cold from my concrete floor. No, the eruption came only from number one. How could it be any different? The eldest of a psychotic mother, who herself had been the eldest under a psychotic mother. That was precisely what I had feared for much of my life. With a few very good friends I shared my worries, my fears. Knowing or suspecting that one day something disastrous would happen. One day, this daughter would do the same. She would destroy herself and her family, her caring husband and her little son. She would destroy her career, her environment and finally herself. This urge to self-destruction is so strong that she would be unable to withstand it. She had been in need of psychiatric help but she had always refused that. She would blame everyone else for her misfortunes. She had worked already many years on that. The whole world was against her. Had we not heard that refrain for decades? And not just from her? It had started with that false accusation of incest, when she was just eleven and after that it had come back every time again in different shape. Now she was almost fifty and her biological transition had been the trigger for the burst. Not much of a provocation had started it. Just a difference of opinion regarding a mutual friend had caused her to explode in anger over the telephone. This was none of my business, she shouted to me. Perhaps so, but it had started when she got upset and wanted to interfere about an agreement I had with said person. That was only the beginning. I was destroying her family. How that so? I had had almost no contact with her and her family.

I had disadvantaged her always since childhood e*t cetera*. And yes, then the never having occurred incest was
brought up again. Did I realize how much trauma I had
caused with that. No, I did not know because it never
happened. I had never touched her nipples (as she had
charged); I had only stroked her back. "Yeah, Papa, do
you know how close that was?" Yes, about six inches and
that with all the clothes on. Trying to fight such statements is well-nigh impossible. Truth is not important;
only her sentiments counted. This was one telephone
call but it was soon followed by another one from her.
She wanted to have nothing to do with me anymore.
No contacts and also no contacts with my grandson.
She was trying to teach me a lesson. She said she would
see me in the Netherlands and then there would be
something happening.

LX

Revenge

I wasn't even extra saddened or so. Something had happened that I had seen coming for years; it was more a sense of acceptance that came over me. I certainly was not going to do anything to try and influence the conduct of number one daughter. She would undoubtedly do her best to tell my other daughters how bad I was, but I hoped that these would have grown suspicious of the regular antics of their older sister. As far as I was concerned I was finished with her. Of course, she was still my daughter. If she ever would get into trouble I would certainly try to help her. The question was whether I would get the chance. In the meantime I had very well heard her threatening words. I knew when she would be in the Netherlands again for a scientific Symposium. I decided to make myself invisible and unfindable for those days. Nothing would be gained by a confrontation. In my town of birth I was house-sitting while the owners were on holidays.

When the doorbell rang I opened the door, totally not expecting anything. There, in the light of a garden lantern, stood my eldest. I was surprised that she had managed to find me.

"What are you doing here?"
"I am here to finish the job where mama failed".

And at the same time I saw how she raised her right arm. Something flashed in the scarce light of the lantern. However, right away my left hand had gone up. I heard a tearing sound and I felt a shoot of pain in that hand. A knife had penetrated my hand palm and the point of the knife was sticking through. My training as a commando made also my right arm go forward and the side of that hand came down on the elbow of her stretched-out right arm. I heard a dry crack and with a yell she let go. Then I saw the knife. The knife with the wavy grip and the black-and-white layers of hard plastic …… She fell down in a corner, while she held her elbow. That right arm was hanging down in a wrong way. She moaned with high-pitched screams. I was also crying. Not because of any pain but rather of pure misery. Now I had to call the alarm number 911. After all those years. I left the knife in my hand; if I pulled it out it would certainly start bleeding even worse. With my right hand I searched in my left vest pocket for my cell phone.

"9…1…1…."
"What the hell are you doing now Gus?" I was screaming to myself.
"You idiot. You are home, boy, you are in Brabant".

Now the tears came in a stream and my glasses filled with them. I shoved the glasses high, but without the glasses I don't see much. I had to bend closely over to see the numbers. The tears splattered like a Spring rain on my phone. My fingers slowly found their goal:

"1…1…2… and now the little green phone".

Gréselle July 2011
Laroque-Gageac June 2014
Amersfoort July 2018